T0063551

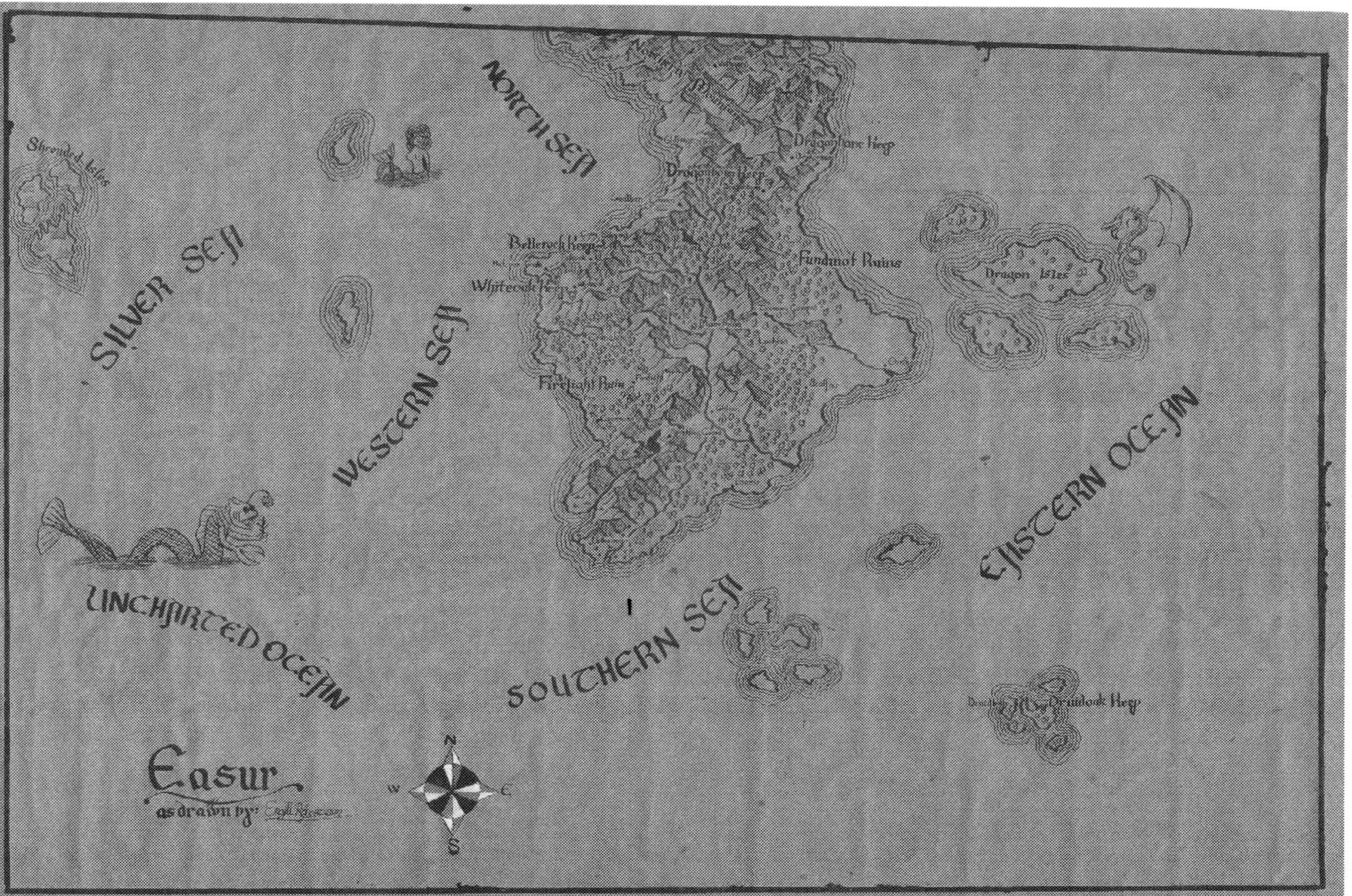

Shrouded Isles
SILVER SEA
NORTH SEA
Bellerock Keep
Fundmot Ruins
Dragon Isles
WESTERN SEA
Firelight Ruin
UNCHARTED OCEAN
SOUTHERN SEA
EASTERN OCEAN
N
W
E
S
Easur
as drawn by:

Memories Lost, Regained

Damarians

Book II

Jessica Rhudolph

Order this book online at www.trafford.com
or email orders@trafford.com

Most Trafford titles are also available at major online book retailers.

Print information available on the last page.

ISBN: 978-1-4907-7127-4 (sc)
ISBN: 978-1-4907-7129-8 (hc)
ISBN: 978-1-4907-7128-1 (e)

Library of Congress Control Number: 2016903844

Trafford rev. 03/04/2016

www.trafford.com

North America & international
toll-free: 1 888 232 4444 (USA & Canada)
fax: 812 355 4082

This book is dedicated to thos who contine to encourage and suport me in my efforts as well as to my children. Thank you i hope you enjoy reading as much as i enjoyed writing.

Introduction

"I be Wynwillow DruidOak lad, an i dunna ken where ye think ye are, but ye be on Easur now an we be almost ta me home. i suggest ye be forth comin an honest lest ye make some enemys ye'd mun rather no"

An anger burned deep inside of him, never had anyone ever spoken to him in such a rude and direct manner, he was both shocked and furious, his hand shot out almost instinctively as he intended to burn her ship to the waterline, murmering the correct words in his fey tongue.

as a sudden hot wind blew from his hands, and yet which grew was nothing like he originally intended, for it was not fire which climbed the walls of her cabin but instead vines with flowers of every color budding on them, the beings eyes turned curiously from her to his hand as he began to shake it like a broken tool.

The look of anger quickly going to that of perplexion. "I am Arnwyn, Crown Prince of the Fey realms. He attempted to summon a flame in his hand no longer caring about what sort of predicament he was in, a cry of horror escaped his lips as a rose grew in his hand.

Chapter 1

Wynwillow watched Adewen moving about the tavern she had to be getting close to her time and Wyn was staying near at hand for when it was she hadnt taken any cargo to Easur sending her crew on ahead instead with out her to make the runs.

She knew Honnora and Rhannon among others were probalby wondering where she was and why she hadnt made the trips as ushual, but Wyn didnt like the thought of Ade being on her own when the babies came.

Wynwillow knew Adewen was setting up a place for them to live on earth a keep with plenty of space and room for little ones to play and run including a garden and more.

Wyn even liked it, Why Ade didnt just use the keep she grew up in on earth with her mother Wyn didnt know but it wasnt for her to decide she herself prefered WhiteOak on Easur if any one specific place.

Nothing like the smell of the sea air.. and Wyn was slowly getting accustomed to leading more than her crew getting to know the other DruidOaksn as well as other clans on Easur.

Not many had made it threw it all but enough that they were able to begin rebuilding. It had been 12 years sence Idrialla's death. It was a pitty that Arion a lone Lycon Adewen had fallen for.

Had gone his own way after finding out Ade was with child. Arion was the last of his pack, and tho he had loved Adewen he could not remain settled in one place hunted by other packs.

due to the differances his own had had. Saying only he hoped in his leaving that the child Ade carried would be thought another half breed regular Lycon Damarian cross, as to apart of his get.

Arion's pack was hunted by the other lycons because they carried special extra gifts in there blood lines. They had been one of few packs feared by there abilitys to see and speak with the dead.

As well as manipulate there auras to better blend in among humans, or use the aura manipulation as a means of armamincy to attack with. However there was also the greater chance that a lycon with these skills would run mad before learning to control them.

Wyn had done her best to help Adewen when ever she could tho to watch her one wouldnt guess she felt his loss as she looked forward to the younglings arrival dispite there not having a father..

Adewen moved slowly about the tavern stepping behind the bar she removed her wepons placing them out of sight but with in easy reach should she need them she was glad Wyn was staying close.

She knew she was worried. Hell... Adewen was worried never having had children before now, but Wynwillow's presents lately was of great comfort. She still ran the tavern and cooked but she couldnt have done it all with out Lilly and Anna.

They were two serving elves who had helped her run the tavern before her mothers death and had stayed on these many years after, and were understanding of her temper lately. Which hadnt been the best her back ached all the time and her tempter was shorter than Wyns on occasion which said alot.

....

Rhannon BelleRock was 5ft 4 in 110lbs soaking wet a full blooded damarian with demon bat like wings horns and tail was a mixture of color her furry fox like body a darker blue black and white than what that of others her wings white and grey.

With large green eyes her hair a light blue leaning more twords teal in color fell about her sholders. She dressed in brown leggings.

a white top belted around her middle just under her breasts with a wide peace of leather that held her top in place she prefered going bare foot so she could move sliently.

Rhannon weilded fire as her element, and was a crafter/ blacksmith for her clan as well as its head of house, and council member for the BelleRock family branch. Her wepons of choice two swords of iorn inlayed with silver.

Carried in sheaths at each hip she along with others had been freed when Idrialla Adewen, Wynwillow, and so many others had returned to Easur, and taking them a few at a time to the earthly realm to retrain in there skills so that they could fight.

Rhannon had hated idri, and the others at first both greatful to be freed, and resentful that idri and the others had not come back for them sooner.

Watching idri and getting to know her as well as the others Rhannon soon grew to admire idrialla, her courage and sacrifice coupled with her intellegence and calm way of listining to everything and everyone before setting her plans into actions, was what eventually won Rhannon over, her death had been a tragic loss.

Rhannons only regret now was not knowing her longer. Her attention now was on her family branch as she begain rebuilding the BelleRock keep, and Village. Making room for the few of the BelleRocks that remained, but as Ade Idri Aune and others had survived to escaped she hoped now that Easur was free others would begin to return home as well.

Rhannon like the rest of her people hated slavery and chains as did many Damarians having woken up from the innital invasion in them. The chains had been enchanted so that they had no use of there abilits.

They couldnt heal one another they couldnt use there element and they couldnt shift shape.. They were held in there true forms that part being the only comforting thing about there captivity but they had been helpless as a human in bondage Rhannon vowed never again she like many others would rather die..

The sound of a hammer strinking steel on an anvel could be heard threw out the keep as Rhannon worked long hours into the night with the help of Aden, along with many others.

Rhannon raised the yonger Bellerocks. Terrock Jaden Sheara Tela Braden Kara and Meela.. Rhannon didnt just make repaires to Bellerock tho it was her first priority she made repairs to all the keeps.

Honnora of the Whiteoaks, and many of her people helped to teach the young what they remembered of reading and writting along with growing crops in the small open valley beneath the cliff there keep sat upon.

Helping Rhannon as much as she could by gathering materials together and had already with the suplies. Wynwillow sent such as seeds from earth for crops and other such things begun providing the extra variaty in the foods produced as well as quantaity to distribute it to each of the keeps.

The DruidOaks doing similar things such as providing fish and other foods from the sea. The Dragonbanes aiding Adewen in training the young.. along with hunting the vast forrested areas of Easur.

As did the Firelights who worked tanning and the weaving of cloth and wool. Each Branch and Keep pulled together working to help one another thrive once more.

The Bellerocks mined the caverns for crystals and other ores that could be used for crafting as well as forge work and were suplied wood as well as tember from the DragonBanes.

While the WhiteOaks taught reading writting, poetry and song, as well as grew vegatables and grains.

Rhannon mostly stuck to her skill set smithing and carpentry. When the younglings she cared for were old enough she would begin extra training sessions with them in arms and in there elements. she hoped they would never have to use them but they had lerned better to be safe and prepaired than sorry.

Never again would they be caught un aware's Rhannon also begain coming up with ways they could in hance the smaller crystals and use a freqincy or tone to send an s.o.s singnal to one another should there ever be a need.

Adewen accepted the responcability of training of her adopted brother Ori and sisters Eva and Rina tho none had really heard much about them as they kept mostly to themselves, following there own persutes and lives till the end of there days. That however is another tale, however they were welcome to Easur.

Ori she knew was stuck on Easur something had happened to him so that he could not return to earth tho Rhannon didnt know what that was or know him well she had seen him wondering off and on simply exploring never really settling in one place or another, he had a home at DragonBorn keep when ever he chose to make use of it.

....

Honnora WhiteOak was 5ft 2in 105 lbs soaking wet antoher full blooded Damarian her furry fox like body actually resembled the coloring of a true fox with its orangy white and black even her eyes looked like orange crystal when her hair didnt hide them from view her hair was long falling to the middle of her back just past her sholders blondie almost white in color tapering to a darker orange at the tips.

like Rhannon she prefered to go barefoot but was the more silent of the two speaking only when necessary she had been threw hell as had others but Honora held the scars of whip marks upon her back not from one whiping but from sevral.

As well as scars upon her wrists and ankles from her many attempts to escape over and over again she kept to her self for the most part tho she she was leader of what was left of the White Oak clan or family branch.

Honnora was dressed in green and brown journaymen's clothing she weilded two daggers and a bow. She had regained many of her abilitys such as healing and shapeshifting.

However her element had not returned to her many speculated that it was because she had fought so much against the enchanted shackles, and demons when in captivity that they had some how stolen her element from her.

So she endevored to aid in other ways and to learn to fight with other wepons. Her horns were black and shot threw with orange streeks, her wings a lighter orange leaning more twords tan in coloring.

Honnora before the invasion had loved to sing and help others. She still helped but she no longer sang at least not where anyone could hear her. her people had been poets healers and song writers as well as warriors..

one day she hoped would be so again for now they provided what aid they could helping her friend Rhannon and the other keeps. She had spoken with wyn as well as the other council members about setting up a sort of market day each month where they could trade.

As well as perhaps set up a festival of sorts in future along with having some dances to begin celebrating life and the future rather than continuing to morn the past it would always be with them with her, and never forgotten but it was time to move forward.

Honnora arrived at BelleRock she knew where to find Rhannon as the sound of her working eccoed threw out the keep. She watched her friend from the door for a bit. Gaining Rhannons attention while she worked was tricky buisness Aden had let her in.

“Rhannon! Rhannon!” Honnora called trying to get above the noise in the end she had to wait for Rhannon to catch Honnora’s scent and look in her direction.

Rhannon did indeed catch Honnora’s scent and stopped what she was doing for the time being frowning at her work thinking shed need to start the peace over anyway.

“Greetings Honnora of the WhiteOaks welcome to what do i owe your visit this eve ? “ Rhannon asked whipping her hands on her aprion and bowing politely to Honnora as one head of house to another.

Honnora bowed in return. “ Thank you Rhannon of the BelleRocks its an honor to be welcome in your home.. however you owe this visit to my concern for Wynwillow of the DruidOaks she has not returned with these last 3 months tho her crew still brings shipments.”

“indeed it is something that should be investagated are you suggesting myself or you go to see what is happining.. ? “ Rhannon asked only a slight peek of interest in her eyes about something other than her work entering it. She remembered stories that Wyn had told them of this Earth. Honnora looked at her simply stating “ i am..”

“When do you perpose to leave we must make arrangements for our house holds before going as heads of house we cannot simply up and go..”

Honnora simply gave her a look and Rhannon grinned her green eyes meeting Honnora's orangey ones holding up her hands in a sign of peace "alright so its not that difficult. Aden can take charge here until we return and knowing you. you've already asked Riaden to take charge"

At Honnoras nod of agreement Rhannon shook her head and glanced back at the peace of metal she'd been working with thinking about how to work it as she absently stated. " well leave in the morning im not waking Aden now especally as the younglings are already asleep."

Honnora had walked furhter into Rhannon's work room standing at the end of one of her work tables hands on hips as she looked at her getting ready to argue the point.

She knew if Rhannon got back to work all else was forgotten. She and Rhannon turned twords the door way at the same time both catching Aden's scent as he joined them bowing respectfully to the heads of house present.

"Acutally Lady Rhannon if i may i apologiese for listining in, but i am awake and tho ive no real liking for Lady Wynwillow for personal reasons. It is of some concern that she has not yet returned with her crew."

"it should be looked into. Her efforts as well as Adewen's in providing supplies from Earth are imortant to all of us. i can mannage here if the two of you wish to leave right away. If i may also suggest it is possable she is assisting lady Adewen with the birthing of her younglings, and Adewen would have sent word were something amiss still lady Honnora is correct in that we should check to be sure."

Rhannon's arms crossed over her chest while she didnt aprove of the eves dropping she did know he ment well after all it was mostly Aden and herself with the aid of a few other remiaining adults.

Looking out for the little ones here at BelleRock and Aden was older than she was by rights should be leader however he had not wished to do so and had allowed her to take his place.

“Thank you Aden we shall indeed go at once” looking over at Honnora she said “ allow me to wash up a bit and ill join you” Honnora nodded in agreement and bowed in thanks not speaking but indicating with her actions she would wait.

“If you will follow me lady Honnora i will show you where you may wait” Aden said rising from his own bow to face her. Honnora nodded in agreement gave Rhannon a hug and then followd Aden.

Rhannon watched them go shaking her head and smiling she had returned Honnora’s hug this would be interesting nether of them had been to earth before. Rhannon reluctently left her work room and made her way up to her own chamber to wash.

....

Wynwillow back at Adewens Tavern on Earth looked up as Vaul enetered.” Talkin er drinkin this eve lad ?”

Vaul looked over at her a rather bland expression on his features rather than his ushual prideful air and assurity tho it was still there there was something else as well troubling him as he spoke “ i think just conversing and relaxing would be best for tonight im not in the right frame of mind for much”

Wynwillow nodded to him as she spoke “no a problem me frien would ye like ta try a new drink i came up wi ? tis called Crystal Fire brewed on Easur.”

“my apollogies for such Lady Wyn im a tad stressed.” The fiend grins and strokes his stubbed chin as he thought over her words seemingly shaking himself from what ever thoughts had been pleauging him. “Twould be a utter delight my dear friend to try that which you offer”

“i distribute it ta Ade’s tavern here on earth an a few other realms such as tha Nova Paw systems “ she smiles walking behind the bar to open a hidden compartment pulling out a bottle made of blue crystal, and getting two glass's from the bar counter. Walking back around glass's in one hand held between fingers bottle in other hand " pick a spot me friend, an les ha a go."

The young in appearance fiend smirks choosing the center stool of the bar resting his elbows upon the wood, resting his chin upon his hands smiling as he watches the preperation and making of the drink. "im curious is the flavor comparable to human experience or is it a treat that transends mortal experience?"

"Transends Ade asures me tis knocked morn a few dwarves on there arses an en mad a dragon er two a bit tipsy after one er two shots " she chuckles happily pooring the drink the liquid is a pale light blue nearly the color of wyns fur.

Her pink colored eyes dance with the light and humor of her statement. The bottle itself a darker color of blue than wyn's wings like cut saphire. The scent of the drink was that of one of the flowers of Easur.

A honey created of the pollen from one of the many plants of Easur added to the liqure. Along with Ceyanne pepper spice blending into the mixture.

After pooring the drinks she put the stopper back in the bottle and set it on the counter between them picking up her glass as if to toast.

"Bottom's up Vaul, i am quite proud o this drink ifn i do say so meself " and she was it was like a combination of the humans rum, and whisky made from corn grown on Easur and some other added ingredeants it was smooth going down, but then the fire hit making one flush and the world would feel as if it were spinning round..

"ta long lastin friendships may they ner fail no matter the bumps alon lifes road.." with that she downed her drink sitting the glass on the counter before the effects kicked in for it wouldnt take long.

Vaul grins and grips the offered drink firmly in hand lifting it up slowly to his pale grey lips holding it there for just a few seconds before suddenly shifts back his head and opens wide his mouth.

Pouring the content offered to him to be chuged in one great gulp it was cool, and smooth just as Wyn had described, and left a pungent taste down his throat as he set it down with a pleased sigh.

Feeling the intense kick after a few seconds that made his eyes widen for a brief instant before he shuttered then sat again with his usual posture grinning mischiviously at her. “indeed quite a kick but its not the most intense drink thats passed these lips since my travels of the worlds described by the ancient viking cultures”

laughing allowed she said “aye indeed the vikins do indeed make a fantastic brew i tho about speakin ta one o the jarels but i doubt en me silver tougne an barterin skills would gain me there secrets “grining she shrugged continueing on “ still twould be fun ta try. another ? “ she asked reaching for the bottle.

“no no my dear friend not a drink you would need to barter for to be brutaly honest the drink with the hardest kick was actualy river water from niflhiem” he grins playfully slaping his right palm onto his own forhead “and my word what a kick that black water has I had nearly named my self the emperor of a village of gnomes before I realized how messed up my mind was”

Wyn contined to grin happily listining to Vaul she put her hand down in her lap not needing another drink enjoying a splended buzz from the one shed already had as well as Vauls company.

“Tis been far too lon sense we ha done this we should mur often.. tell m me where ha ye been an o yer travels these last two years sense idris death.. Ades nearly ready ta ha her twins ye ken.. been stayin close as she ha no other family near ta hand ta aid her. Well asside her Ookami pack bu they ha there own concerns an dunna ha the time a persent ta be o aid unless she went ta stay wi in the pack.”

“I was even wearing a crown made of a bunch of pointy hats tied together and was wearing crimson wool pijama’s for Pride’s sake! I dont even remember how I had gotten those cloths of even how I left niflheim!”

Wynwillow chuckles reolizing the drink had more of an effect on him then he had yet to notice as he rambled on.

“Iv been traversing the other worldy realms with an essance of any type that is comparable to my own which lead me to travserve the more wicked worlds of the Norse world tree, as well as a few less notable such plains”

Wynwillow raises an eyebrown tilting her head curiously wondering if he had been pestering the Asguard.” interstin an i may be a wee bit tipsy me friend but im no so drunk ive lost me wits yer bein awfuly veg...how er ill no press yer secrets be yer own.

She stood and leanded against the counter as they talked still facing him but watchful and ever mindful of there surroundings. It was late enough that very few humans were out this late unless it were soldjers or thos returning home from some elete party of one sort or another.

“tis no secret my friend but some worlds have no name that would make sense to you or many mortals.” He grins feeling only a slight tingle in the back of his mind from the drink shaking his head lightly “and my sincere congradulations on Adewens up coming birth of the twins”

Wynwillow smiled softly at the thought of Ade and her twins to be tho she was also concerned for her. “aye she be looking forward ta them im in no hurra meself ta ha any. She be on her own Arion no bein aroun now rouge lycons dunna settle tho in his way i thin he loves her still.. Ade will be a fine mum no matter..”

“aye her caring manner makes her a very fine mother to be sure.” He grins and leans back on the stool again stroking his stuble as he closes his eyes his mind awander within his fond memeories of adventures in days long past.

“aye.. well me friend i must be off fer the ev i needs check in on Ade an then see about prepairn the next shipment ta Easur tryin ta keep Adewen from the tavern this close ta her time is no an easy task en fer me “ Wyn chuckles placing a freindly hand on Vauls sholder “ Dunna be a stranger ye ken.. else ill track ye down an gi ye what fer”

“As you say Lady Wyn I shall attempt to visit more frequently from this point forward” he smiles at his long time friend. “take care of your self and lady adewen alright?”

“Aye. i shall ye can count on tha.. “ Wynwillow leaned in and kissed Vauls cheek grinning cheekly fairly skipping out the door.

Chapter 2

Ade Damn an blast ye! i told ye ta stay home ye dunna belong here, sa close ta yer time..! " Wynwilllow called out looking quite angry as Adewen walked inside wyn hopped over the bar counter and begain to advance twords her.

Adewen stood her ground she like Wyn was in human form when on Earth. Wynwillow was dressed in a burgendy pirate like outfit rather than her ushual blue. Adewen in a dark blue gown with silver threaded brocade Wyns hair was pulled back in a brade while Adewens long white flowed down her back nearly to her knees almost grown fully back down to her ankles.

"its good to see you too Wyn and i m sorry but i cant stay home and just wait around i grow restless and anchious i cant do it. especally as it could be days or weeks yet before its time " adewen replyed to wyn as she drew near enough to be heard with out shouting over minstrials music and patrons laughter.

All seemed to be going well the aroma of food cooking and ale or other drinks filling the air Ade could tell Wyn had things well in hand and had to grin knowing it was ether Lilly or Anna cooking because Wyn couldnt even boil water.

“i dunna gi a rats arse yer goin home en if i ha ta take ye back me self. Ye look tired an i ken tell yer hurtin, but tryin no ta say anythin su dunna argue lets go..” Adewen grinned at her and nodded part of her wanted to cry and tears did threaten to spill but she was able to grin because she knew Wynwillows frustration and anger at her was out of concern.

“alright alright well go “ Adewen said raising her hands in a sign of defete and peace for th time being. Her back did ached nearly all the time now and the ride here hadnt done it any favors. She did need to sit down, and did so while wyn went out to bring the horse and carrage back around from the stables.

Wynwillow walked away gave ordes to Lilly and Anna as well as a few others it was hard not to laugh at because Wyn sounded like she was giving orders to her crew rather than simply speaking with them as Adewen did.

It seemed in its own way they both recived results in some fashion. As soon as Wynwillow came back inside she arose and walked with her and got into the cart Wyn taking up the regns drove. After a few miles Adewens voice could be heard “ Wyn..”

“Aye ? Ade what is it ? “ Wyn asked payin attenion to the road as she guided the horse trying to make the ride as smooth as possable..” you may want to go faster i .. i think its time”

There was pain in Ades voice and about the time Wynwillow looked over at her Adewens water broke. Wyn if possable looked even paler than she already was and then angry and then worried. “ BLOODY HELL ! Hold on tight. ill get ye home”

Wyn whiped the horse into a faster pace flying down the road gudiding it over the ruts and pathways to the keep cursing the whole way reminding Ade and herself to breath that they would be there soon.

Wyn pulled up infront of the keep jumping down from the wagon and going round to the side Ade was on she did not waist time as soon as Adewen was down from the cart she lifted her in her arms.

Not carring who might see or that she was getting wet from where ades gown brushed against her she carried her to her room and helped her change into a clean gown.

Adewen cryed out in pain as the contractions were painful Wyn helped her onto the bed.." breath Ade dunna push no yet just hold onta the bed post an breath.."

Adewen gave wyn a look that if looks could kill Wynwillow knew she would have dropped on the spot wyn chuckled a bit at it, and set about tending the horse and cart as well as gathering everything she was going to need.

it would be hours yet before thos wee ones were ready to push into this world which gave her the time she needed.

She set water to heat for bathing Adewen and the little ones after as well as blankets clean sheets and bedding among other things such as washing her own hands and arms and cleaning her dagger prepairing it for cutting the ambilical cords.

Wyn checked on Ade constantly threw out gathering everything her jacket gone and her sleeves rolled up Wyn helped Ade move to the edge of the bed .." aright Ade love here we be.. breath" Wyn knelt between her legs putting Adewen's feet one on each sholder " aright lass push.."

....

Honnora and Rhannon arrived on earth with Wynwillows crew having traveled with them they tracked Wynwillow and Adewen by scent to Adewens keep each taking on a human form so as not to frighten anyone.

They knew from Wynwillow's stories and so forth about Earth that it was better to blend in as much as possable. They arrived at the keep just as Adewen pushed out the first little girl.

They had rushed up the stairs hearing Adewens screams, and curses as she yelled at Wyn.. Rhannon was blond haired and green eyed while in human form Honnora was red headed and her eyes remained orenge in coloring.

Upon entering the room Wyn looked at them and begain giving orders Rhannon was directed to help suport Ade, and talk to her keep her breathing while Honnora was handed the first little one wrapping her in a blanket.

Wyn cleared her airway and knotted the cord before cutting it. Handing the baby to Honnora who looked at Wyn as if she were nuts but carefully held the little one as Wyn turned back to assist with the second..

Together all three helped Ade deliver the younglings... the first born was Named Idrialla after her grandmother who passed, and the second Lillianna both were beautiful.

The first had the purple and blue gem like eyes that marked her Dragonborn herratage the second had her fathers eye coloring of sky blue they were non identical twins.

Idri being white in color like her father with no wings. Lillianna red, and black with Wings sadly little Lillianna did not survive the birthing. Thus little idri was the only child born much to Adewen's sorrow.

Wynwillow remained with her for months helping to tend the child an pull Ade from her greif Honnora and Rhannon remained as well taking turns until they had to return to Easur to see to ther duties as heads of there own houses.

Adewen returned as much to her old self as she was able turnning her attention to her one remaining child, taking her to Easur to raise her bringing her to earth once a month durring the full moons and to tend the taverns affairs as needed.

Wyn too returned to her duties as head of house and merchent transporting cargo between the realms training Killian and other Druidoaks how to sail the ships so that when they were old enough and able they too could transvers the realms with supplies for trade.

....

a year passed with Adewen returning to running her tavern and traveling back and forth from Earth to Easur as needed to tend to matters of council and so forth, she was now on Earth awaiting Wynwillows arrival, the day was warm and the sea calm a slight breeze but nothing more.

She had found a guardian for little idir so that she wouldnt have to travel with her quite as much he was a Dragon by the name of Wolfen and connected to there friend Devon Stormbringer.

Wynwillow was returning to earth with a shipment of crystal fire from Easur and a shipment of wine from the Novapaw realm where ther friend and Ally Storm hailed from, to store at Adewen's keep for a few days before moving the alcohol to the tavern. Ade was to meet them at the Isles Wyn had helped establish years ago.

Wynwillows ship the Gypsy Dragon appeared threw a rift in the realms a swirl of pink and purple portal energy opening to allow the ship threw it was smoking, and on fire another ship closing in on her as Wyn yelled orders to the crew she turned the ship round broad side so that she could fire her cannons ..

As the rift closed behind the other ship Wyn's guns fired both cannon balls and electric like shocks bolts of energy shot from the crystal that helped power the ship. Wyn having ordered the power converted from shielding to weapons. The shields didn't protect against attack but held the ship together when traveling through the rifts.

The cannons shooting would sound like bombs going off or repeated bangs of thunder but too rapid to truly be called such the bell below in the island village would ring loudly for there people to take cover they knew cannon fire when they heard it..

Wyn's ship had taken some damage but the other was taking even more as it was hit with some blue electric like energy streaming from the crystals on wyn's ship causing a lot of damage to its hull while it turned so that it could return fire.

Wyn called for the crew to reload, and alternate between cannon and power shots from the crystal so that while one was loading the other was shooting and while one was charging the other firing.

The other ship fired again getting a lucky shot in at the crystal .. Wyn called out for the crew to fire hitting the other ship again. Doing more damage but not quiet enough to make her go down.. Wyn's ship was dead in the air so to speak with the crystal gone she called for the crew to draw there swords as the other ship began to board.

"CUT THE LINES! " she called using her wind ability's to fill the sails and attempt to maneuver the ship away from the other.. the crew cut the lines some of the pirates having made it over and engaged in sword play but not many steel meeting steel rang out the bells from the village stopped ringing as all the villagers had made there way to the caves for safety..

Wyn recognized the captain and the ship that was attempting to board her it was the Celsius.. none of the old crew she had known remained save the bastard catnip who had wanted a darker name for himself that had left her ashore.. in many ways he had done her a favor.. but now that Wynwillow knew the old crew was no more she had no compunctions against ending his life or destroying his ship.

Adewen in human form had been collecting shells on the beach to make a mobile for her little Idri. Wyn had contacted her earlier and let her know she would be arriving and so was waiting for Wyn's return. She heard the sound of cannon fire and the bells of the village begin to ring with alarm.

She looked up into the sky her silvery eyes widening as she saw Wynwillow's ship turn broadside to fire on another as the rift closed behind them one of the cannon balls fired from the other ship, and missed.

Adewen diveded aside into the water the cannon ball landing in the sand mere inches from where she had been standing sending sand exploding in several directions leaving a small crater in the sand bar. as Ade surfaced from the water swimming back twords shore she changed shape to her true form going skyward.

The pirate captain boarded her ship before she got it away from his, and advanced Wyn called for her crew to abandon ship the minute she stopped powering the sails with her ability's the ship would go down and crash into the water her crew did as ordered.

Wynwillow drew her sword holding the ship long enough to make sure her crew what was left made it to the life rafts, or as they were low enough over the water dived for it.. her blade met the other captains and the ship began to go down " well well we meet again little Wyn " Wyn smirked " so we do.. what did ye do wi the old crew?"

He parried and spun dropping low bringing his blade down aiming for the back of her legs Wyn did a back wards hand spring kicking him in the jaw in the process.. he let out a yell at the same time some of his crew advanced t words one of the crews boats that had gotten stuck.

Wyn came up out of her hand spring and threw her sword cutting the line that held the dingy in place sending it skidding down to the water below. The other captain realizing her ship was going down lept back to his own, but not before taking advantage of Wyn's distraction.

When she threw her blade he also cut a rope that was attached to the sail and ducked letting the sail swing round to catch Wyn in the side knocking her down. Pinning her to the side of the ship.

Stuck under its weight as the ship sank with the smoke from the fire no one could see clearly who all had managed to escape and who had not.. but it was clear the Gypsy had lost this skirmish.

Adewen flew words the ship reaching it as the pirate captain leap back to his own ship. She looked for Wyn but didn't see her on the deck one of the lines to the sails had turned and struck the side of the ship but its canvas and the smoke had hidden Wyn from view.

As the ship went down Ade assumed Wyn had escaped with the crew.. so called lighting to her hands to strike the other ships sails so that it would have no choice but to put down in the water, or crash slowing its escape.

Ade then flew low along the water searching out Wyn's crew men who had dived in getting them to safety as well as manipulating the water so the life boats would be safely out of the way when the ship hit the water.

Wyn still pinned against the side of the ship was out for moments before the pain woke her almost instantly the canvas indeed hiding her from view a few of her ribs had cracked upon the beam's impact.

The lower part of the ship crashed into the ground first the front part tilting forward into a sort of nose dive as it hit the water jarring the ship splitting the bottom half of it from the top half.

The crystal what was left of it would shatter beneath the weight of the upper part of the ship the jarring would knock the beam off of Wyn and send her sliding up against one of the cannons.

Wyn cursed the pain in her side and head struggling to her feet using her wind ability to push the canvass of the sail away from her so she could see. smoke stung her eyes she had to get off the ship before the fire reached the gunpowder.

The crystals powering the ship cracked and shattered the ship started to creak and moan as it tilted words the sand bar about to be lay ed on its side.

Adewen watched the ship crash and looked around her for Wyn knowing she must be heart broken at the loss of the Gypsy Dragon, but didn't see her. worried she called to the sailors Wyn's crew to get to the caves with the villagers and remain there it was the safest place she could think for them to be.

It was then that she noticed the sail the can vice of the ship flipping backwards that she saw Wyn still on deck and thought by the gods she wont make it in time.. Ade took off words the ship hoping to reach Wyn before the ship exploded.

Wyn's eyes opened slowly seeing the ship sink and where the fire was spreading too Wyn knew she had to get off the ship and fast she saw Ade flying words her and yelled "NO! STAY BACK !"

Wynwillow ran for the edge of the ship, ignoring the staggering pain in her ribs, barely having enough time to reach the edge of the railing leaping up on top of it and dive into the water.

She screamed from the pain it caused her ribs then quickly held her breath as she hit the water she didn't waist any energy shifting forms, not to mention the pain that would also cause at the moment.

The pirate captain stood on the deck of his ship the only decent thing he had done seance taking it over would be to go down fighting with it he turned his own ship around on the water now its mast still on fire.

He aimed his own cannons trying to hit Wyn's crew his only satisfaction before he died would be in knowing he had taken out the Gypsy Dragon, and the only one left of the old crew if he couldn't get the secret none would not knowing Wyn was still alive.

Ade heard Wyn warning yell and stayed back watching horrified while Wyn dove into the water as the Gypsy exploded Adewen was still far enough back that she was unharmed.

The debris and peaces of wood and crystal from the ship rained down around them, the aftershock and wave that rolled across the area sent her flying end over end backwards for a moment or two before she corrected herself.

Seeing the destruction of the gypsy and Wyn going down with her ship she flew low over the water and changed forms into one of the meridian folk, and swam after Wyn when she didn't surface.

All the animals and other living things had left the area long ago so only the area around where the ships had been would have been effected Wyn struggled to swim with broken ribs and winced when Ade reached her, but didn't fight relaxed instead and let her get her out of the area and to the surface.

Wynwillow took a deep breath when Adewen surfaced with her and drug her to shore there were tears in her eyes at the loss of her ship, but it couldn't be helped. she mumbled something about that ship having cost her a great deal and it would take a good deal of time and effort to find another like it. Looking up at Ade swimming towards land with her she said "Thank ye Lass.."

Ade shook her head and couldn't help grinning over the fact that Wyn was more worried about the loss of her ship than she was about herself but Wyn was a merchant at heart always had been..

"Don't worry you'll get another in time and Easur isn't hurting for supplies any longer its nearly self sustaining .. .. now lets get you ashore and see how bad your injured you didn't change forms when you went into the water"

Wyn frowned " best hurry lass tha ship be com min fer us shortly leave me an finish the basters else heal me quick sa i ken aid ye " Ade nodded swimming faster.

Wynwillow now rested on land soaked and waited for Ade to look over her wounds her side would be black and blue from where the beam had struck she knew the beam had cracked a couple of the ribs, and she was sure she had probably finished breaking them when she dived from the ship into the water.

Every movement hurt like hell but she simply looked towards the ship so she had something else to think about other than the Gypsy's loss and being injured..she tried to keep from sounding like she was in pain and said.

"one.. hell o.. a day... wouldn't ye agree?" Ade glared at her ducking as Wyn pulled her down crying out as she rolled over covering Ade as another cannon shot hit near by, both of them being sprayed with sand.

....

Just off the beach area Vukan sat and watched what he thought was one of his own a Damarian. He hadn't had much luck finding any of his own, and he has followed this one lady knowing she was, but could never find out definitely.

Hearing the cannon fire he watches her manipulate the water giving aid to one of the two ships that had emerged through a rift he hadn't seen that in well over an age, and then sees her shift form.

He is shocked to see he is right his hunch had proved correct. He waits for her to hit the air in her burgundy red form, white hair flowing as her wings flap. she is pretty in Damarian form by both human an Damarian standards.

He continues to watch until she and another are on the ground. it is the other one that intrigue him enough to come forward in his human form addressing them as he kneels and bows in respect.

"I walk before you and kneel as I have watched you and since changing form you have made my day, I am Vukan of Firelight " as he finished speaking he changes from human to Damarian form " may i help?"

Wynwillow, and Adewen both look looked up from Wyn having had pulled Adewen down to rolled over on top of her covering her head both pairs of eyes one of Silver, and one of Pink met his.

"Are ye bloody daft ge down a fore ye get shot.. " the ship was close enough now that the crew was loading pistols to be fired at them as well as cannons. Adewen smiled helping Wyn off her while saying.

"yes your help would be most welcome i am Adewen Dragonborn, and this is Wynwillow Drudoak.. Wynwillow if you don't hold still so i can heal you i am going to knock you out " Wyn glared at Ade.

"i dare ye ta try, broken ribs er no ill kick yer arise Ade, this be no damn time fer pleasantry an introductions tis time fer action an if in ye canna ge a move on ill do it me self " Wyn gritted her teeth glaring at them a second and tried to get up. Dispite her broken ribs.

Ade grinned knowing Wyn just needed something to distract her from the pain, and her temper was the easy out let.." Can you heal her while i finish of that ship, and crew firing at us..?"

laughing at being called daft neither lady knew his kneeling was to communicate with the earth as he finds the ship above the earth in the water. He concentrates his gaze locks onto the one with pink eyes, the one injured. knowing she is another Damarian whose beauty he has never seen the likes of, not knowing who she is or why she is injured he gets very angry.

Refocusing he pushes up the earth, sand and ground beneath the ship the earth answering. Vukan his hands giving off a soft greenish glow. It races upwards through the water finding the ship it shoves it up, and out of the water as tendrils of sand reach up on either side along the ship then shoots downwards to the deck each side pulling out words.

Eventually ripping the ship in two along the keel as the wood splinters, shatters under the force of the sand, and earth beneath it. Leaving the ship split on a column of earth 50 feet in the air. Pandemonium through out the ship." I hope that helps for now "as he smiles never leaving his kneeling position.

Adewen felt the earths vibrations she smiled she knew what it was he was doing, and nodded to him impressed. Wyn grinned seeing the ship rising up out of the water its crew diving over the sides as the sand rushed in over the sides tearing it apart.

Tho there was still a hard set to her features as if she were thinking very hard about something other than matters at hand she kept an eye out for the captain of that ship to see if he survived or not.

Ade raised Wyn's shirt to look over the injuries Wyn winced, but made no sound her sword still in hand she kept her attention on there surroundings, and the crew of the ship that survived who were making there way to shore..

Adewen looked from Wynwillow's injuries to Vukan. in human form he had been good looking but in Damarian well he was quite dashing he had the same blue coloring as Wyn, but where her fur was white his was black, and his eyes the blue of Easur's crystals.

His hair was long thick wavy black in coloring.. " can you keep them back if they draw to near before i get her healed she'll fight them injured or not.." Wyn cut in glaring, and growling. " I'm no an infant Ade ye need no talk as if i be the daft one.."

Adewen shook her head." At times Wyn i believe you are.." Wyn's grin reached her eyes that time and they danced with as much humor as pain tho she winced as the laughing hurt her ribs " Ge on wi it then Ade love they be cumin.."

Ade nodded and trusted Vukan to see to the pirates advancing upon them she placed her hands on Wynwillow's side she knew Wyn was tense and ready to battle if need be.

Ade closed her silvery eyes and sent part of her spirit seeking inside of Wyn's body her hands began glowing with a soft yellow light as she begin healing Wyn from the inside out repairing the broken ribs and muscle damage.

Oh how he enjoyed hearing what appeared to be two friends as they bicker back and forth and know there is concern as well as care between the two of them. He just looks at the one whom asked if he can handle them.

He knew she felt what he did as her smile told him. Grinning he nods affirmative as he stands striding towards the water without a word, putting himself between the pirates and the ladies.

It has been a bit since he has been able to fight alongside fellow Damarians and inside he is excited as well as mean. He sees the ones who survived making their way to the shore still in the water. knowing he does not want to physically fight after hearing if it comes to that the one injured would fight he was not a very merciful one right now.

He stands in his full form wings outward arms stretched out to his side as he leans his head up concentrating hard pulling energy from the atmosphere especially from the earlier pink and purple energy he knew was still there.

Vukan brought forth a curtain of lightning hitting the water knowing it would electrify the water outward from where it hits and with enough diameter to hit every one of the survivors.

This curtain of lightning lasts for 20 seconds with the crackling, snapping of energy, intensive light. He looks over the water afterwords not seeing a sign of life.

Walking back keeping an eye on the horizon until the ladies are in front of him again. " I believe we have time to heal this one to the point she is no longer in heavy pain. I will keep watch as you do."

Wyn watched the male who had introduced himself as Vukan of the Firelight's as he finished off the pirates with his ability's. only the pirates were harmed by it, as the fish merfolk and other animals would have fled the area long before when the cannons had first begun firing..

Wyn willow concentrated on her breathing, as Adewen repaired the damage even with Damarians healing methods broken ribs being reset hurt like hell,, but still she made no move, or sound simply watched him as he approached them.

Adewen's expression was one of concentration and focus on what she was doing slowly the bruising around Wyn's injuries began to fade and look as tho she had never been injured at all.

"Thank ye Lord Firelight fer yer aid this eve.. tis good ta ken mur o yer folk aside tho's we already ken ha survived " Wyn said when he drew near enough the glow from Adewen's hands faded and her silvery eyes opened. Wyn quickly reached out to catch and steady Ade with her free hand her sword still in the other.

Healing another took a lot of energy to do and if they weren't careful could drain them to the point of passing out leaving them helpless. Wyn waited until she had regained her balance before letting her go then got to her feet scanning there surroundings before re sheathing her blade.

Adewen smiled at Wyn grateful for the assistance and after a few moments was quite alright tho quit hungry she too turned to Vukan.. "thank you for your assistance.. how is it we were fortunate enough you were so close as to give us aid?"

He blushed as both thanked him for his assistance for to him he expected to help other Damarians it was not something he should think about he should just do. " It was nothing and as to what would have me so close. " He pauses as he thinks over the options to tell finally he says.

"I had my suspicions of this lady here " points to Adewen" being Damarian however could not get proof. I followed her to the ocean and was watching as she collected shells. It was fate to see her change form and at that moment I knew. Also I have been searching for my sister, Lila, hoping to find her but as I see you, neither of you are she." he sighs than falls to his knees, beginning to wonder if he would ever find his sister.

"yes as I know right now I am a Firelight and hope not to be the only one after my mother and father were last head of household." looks at both ladies one with pink eyes another with red burgundy skin " You are neither of same household are you? May I ask who I have had the pleasure of meeting?"

Chapter 3

Wynwillow looked at Ade both of them did indeed know Vukan's sister. Tho Lila had gone her own way she was in fact still in this realm that they knew of and on earth. Wyn nodded to Ade who then spoke up. "We know of your sister Vukan. She has been a friend and ally to us for a long while now.

She comes and goes and is in fact here on earth however she's gone out exploring, and isn't expected to return for awhile yet. You should also know if you haven't already heard Easur has been freed as well at great cost"

Adewen pauses thinking of her mother and all the other Damarians that fell. Wyn places a comforting hand on Adewen's solder knowing where her thoughts must have turned.

"We are honored ta meet ye Vukan o the Firelights.. ye are correct in tha we ar no o the same family branch.. i am Wynwillow o the Druidoak's and Head o me Family Branch.. an this be Deaden o the Dragonborns."

"now head o her branch as well. would ye care ta join us fer the evenin we ken catch ye up on all thas happened in these last years. yer sister be hale an whole least wise last we saw her as well as a happy lass.."

Vukan is overwhelmed hearing his sisters name said aloud and knowing these two ladies know of her and have seen her. alive his heart soared and emotion came over him. As tears flowed from his eyes and down his cheeks he says with as steady a voice he can manage.

"Yes I would love to spend time speaking with you and hearing about Easur and how things are. I have not heard any news of Easur for quite some time, it would be good to be around other Damarians. " He smiles getting back to his feet" Can I help either of you back to town or wherever you need to get to?"

Wyn nodded and looked out over the sea giving Vukan time to recover himself as tears came to his eyes. Deaden stepped forward brushing the tears from his eyes. " well all fly back together and land just outside the village. We take on human form from there ill sound the all clear Wyn if its alright with you when we get there to let the villagers know its safe again.."

Ade looks over at Wyn seeing her expression Deaden wonders at her thoughts" Wyn..? " Wyn turns back to them her expression having been a serious one before she smiled again.

"Aye let us go dunna worrie Ade i were but mornin me ship an thinkin its gonna take Rhannon an some o the others a wee while ta build another no ta mention Rhannon's tempers about as bad as me own shes gonna be a might pissed as well the Gypsy Dragon be lost."

Grateful for the gesture of one of the ladies, the one named Deaden he believes. he speaks up. " Thank you but these are tears of joy and happiness not of sadness. I am fine and these tears have been waiting to flow. I will follow and be happy to change into human form again to make sure we are not seen."

He gets up and stands in front of these ladies bows hearing they are head of households " It is an honor to meet you both and grateful for you generosity and thoughtfulness." He takes another look out at the water looking to make sure none will follow sees no movement even when he takes to the air to get a better look and see between swells

Wynwillow and Adewen both smile as Vukan speaks and takes to the air they spread there own wings and join him Wyn Flying ahead leading the way her thoughts turning to something she needed to do and hoped when later if she had to explain, Adewen and the others could forgive her.

First she had to be sure it was still where she had put it and if not she would have to track it down, but to do that she would need another ship and it was going to cost her time she couldn't afford..

Her thoughts turned back to the present she smiled for now she would enjoy the company of her friend and there new found friend Vukan. she admired his courage altho she had called him daft not many would walk into a battle like that ignoring cannon fire and offer aid.

Landing just outside the village she took on human form and waited for Vukan and Adewen to arrive Ade flew next to Vukan " tell me of yourself Vukan and your travels if it wont trouble you to do so and please forgive Wyn shes not really as grumpy as she seems once you get to know her you'll she shes really a wonderful woman"

Flying with them he thinks about what just happened. not more than an hour ago he was watching someone picking up sea shells, than he sees transformation and not only one but two. oh that second one with pink eyes is a tough one and damn she is a looker.

He can't believe he thinks that right now but knows his own senses and she is going to be one that will haunt if he doesn't try. He lands and listens to Deaden speak as he changes to human form.

"Adewen, right? It appears we are near and headed into the village I would be happy to tell of my travels however shouldn't I say so in front of the two instead of repeating?"

He laughs at her words regarding Wynwillow. " I will tell you since you seem to be defending her " He points to Wynwillow. " I have no idea of her to be anything other than a wonderful woman.

To take such a beating and still want to fight knowing it would cause more injury and to make sure you are not alone. I would say she actually caught my eye especially with those pink ones of hers."

He shakes head thinking himself a fool after all they didn't know him yet or he them and here he was confessing to one of them this thoughts about the other." For some reason seeing you both and her in particular.

"I had to move and help out regardless of what was going on. I speak to much on this. Shall we continue inside and i will talk if you want. " he gestures for her to lead and waits for her to do so.

Adewen smiled landing beside him and taking on human form listening to all he has to say. " that is true telling your store once would be much better than having to tell it again and again. you are correct in that she is a very brave woman many of us would and have given our selves to protect others."

"even injured she thought to protect me knowing of my little one who is quite safe with her guardian Wolfen. i came to await Wyn's return and saw the shells thinking to use them to make a mobile with them and the crystals."

"so began gathering them. you are also correct i am Adewen please call me Ade on earth we are less formal then on Easur. Easier to blend in. I'm glad she caught your attention" Ade grows quiet knowing as they draw nearer to where Wyn is the easier it will be for them to be heard as Damarians hearing and sense of smell is quite astute.

Wyn turned to face them as they approached in her human form she looked like a dark haired fair skinned elf. Her eyes were the only thing about her that remained the same. she could admit if only to herself as they approached she was more aware of Vukan than she wanted to be at present.

He quite took her breath away tho she gave nothing of these thoughts away in posture or tone he was quite handsome in his way the set of confidence to his angular face he was no youth but a male fully grown and capable of defending himself as well as any other.

She noticed the way his clothing fit the play of his muscles she shook her head and grinned to dispel her wayward thoughts. " ye two er slow Ade sound the bell fer the all clear I'll go ta the tavern an open it ta tho's who will wish a drink er two as well as speak wi a few o the villagers once they come out o the caves behind the falls ta assure them all is well ill meet ye both inside once we've done.."

Ade's silvery eyes meet Wyn's her long white flowing hair held loosely in a thick braid nearly down to her ankles looking a little angry herself as she speaks out. " Wyn i am not one of your crew to be ordered about ill thank you to remember that.."

Wyn had been about to answer Vukan's statement with some sarcastic remark or another when Ade's words reached her ears she tilted her head stopping short at Adewen's tone a slow grin touched her lips as she bowed politely to Ade.

"aye ye are correct Ade i owe ye an apology i fer get me self a times an tend ta take charge en among friends" Ade smiled then accepting the apology and giving her a hug. " well meet you as you said next time just ask.. ill have a pint of rum waiting for you."

Wyn grinned then " ahh now ye ha me attention ill be lookin forward ta tha.." turning to Vukan she answered his question " aye these isles be me home here on earth tho the people here dunna ken I'm a Damarian. Ade brings shipments from the main land here as did i afore me ship were lost."

Adewen left them alone to talk while she went and rang the bell sounding the all clear Wyn began walking as they talked. " The tavern an many o the build ins here as well as the merchant stalls er all built by tho's wish in ta make a home here."

"I'm more what ye would call the peace maker an merchant tha made it possible they be used ta pirate battles bein out here sa far in the sea were one o the few ports open ta all."

Adewen, Wynwillow and Vukan gathered together that evening taking turns telling there tales how they escaped Easurs invasion and met up on earth as well as Ade and Wyn telling of Idrialla's death and how Easur became free once more.. it would be a few months before Wyn would see Vukan again.

....

Rhannon upon finding out about what happened to the Gypsy Dragon was indeed angry with Wyn over its loss givin it had been the first of that kind, and had taken her and others working with her nearly two years to complete.

It took some sweet talking on Wyn's part to gain one of the other three ships Rhannon had built after the Gypsy one was called Orical the other two Onyx and SkyKing, the SkyKing being the largest of the vessals more were in the making.

Wynwillow captined Orical now and begain making her own plans this last trip back to Easur with supplies would be delivered, and then she would set out to check on matters.

First she would needs stop by earth to see what Devon wished of her. She gazed out over the open sky standing near the railing of the ship as WhiteOak hall came into view..

Honnora sat in what was left of the once larger librarry at WhiteOak Hall outside she could hear the yonglings Charrick and Orick outside playing it was summer Riden often took them fishing, or swiming

Jessmena along with Sorandria and Minera took turns seeing to the cooking.

Honnora often along with Roandale taught them how to fight read and write. in the quiet of the evenings they would take turns singing playing music or telling stories with many of the others. Poems and a game called chess that Wyn had taken time to teach them on her visits when she brought shipments.

Honnora didnt sing but she wrote listened and played instriments the younglings came running inside about the time the winds picked up calling out to her. " Honnora a ship Honnora ! its Wyn ! Shes BACK !"

Honnora stood smiling at them as they ran around her desk and walked outside with them about the time Wyns ship pulled up near the cliff WhiteOak rested upon.

WhiteOak looked more like a monastary than a keep there were three buildings surounded by a high wall with cells attatched to two of the buildings where they had been chained no longer were chains in thos cells.. thanks to Rhannons skills in removing them.

Honnora avoided them at all costs as they held some terrable memories for her.

The main building held a living room area with two small rooms off to the side one of which an office and sick room, which doubled as an apothocary .. the other a small bedroom.. once threw the livingroom one entered the library with two larger rooms on ether side of it.

Both of those rooms were bedrooms also. the other two buildings one a bath house the other the kitchens and dinning hall. In the process of being built were more housing an armory and berricks.

Wyn looked out over the railing of her ship as her crew set about lowering its plank and acnchorning off. Wyn didnt wait for the plank however and glided over on her own wings.

Honnora and Wyn met half way once Wyn landed bowing to one another in greeting then giving each other a hug as Wyns crew begain unloading a shipment of cargo that Honnora would distribute threw out the keeps.

Vukan having heard rumor of a ship coming and that it would be around dusk between the two sunsets he ventured off to WhiteOak to see the commotion and to see if he could visit with those about.

His day had been a busy one with doing this and that keeping up the keep meeting Donovan and the rest of the Firelights on Easur that had survived little Nim and Areil as well as an older lad named Adeon, but now it was time to meddle in some trouble.

As he nears WhiteOak he sees indeed a ship has arrived, as he lands in the courtyard he see two talking, by the scent he can tell one he knows, but the other not that familiar.

After landing he walks nearer and greeting them says " It is a fine evening for ones to arrive home. What tales have you brought with you this time, Wyn? " He bows respectfully with a little over dramatic to it laughing to himself.

Wynwillow let go of Honnora grinning as Vukans scent reached them her pink colored eyes danced merrily as he approched and bowed.

Honnora not knowing him took up a defensive posture her orengy gem like eyes glittering with a dangerous light tho her mannor was friendler than it might have been given he was a damarian Honnora nodded to him as he spoke and bowed Wyn feeling Honnoras tension spoke up giving introductions.

"Honnora lass relax he be a friend Adewen an i met him a few months ago he be the one Ade told ye o over the crystals about that gave us aid when me ship were attacked.."

There was a slight chuckle to wyns tone " Honnora WhiteOak allow me ta present Vukan o the Firelights... Vukan Lady Honnora head o the WhiteOak family branch an as fer tales i ha a few"

Looking up as Wynwillow speaks he sees her sparkling pink eyes knowing he has missed seeing them even though he did not dare stare at her eyes months before they are all he can think of know .. putting that aside, Vukan knows his manners and turns while bowed to Lady Honnora.

"My Lady Honnora I am honored to meet with your aquiantance and apologize for my sudden appearance without proper request, appears the excitement of the area seeing Lady Wynwillow arrive is quiet infections " He grins and chuckles a bit in a warm playful manner.

"As stated I am Vukan of Firelights" He kneels as he knows this is way overboard but he did enter as he owned the place without proper introduction to head of household, and waits for permission to get up

Honnora relaxed her guard as Wynwillow spoke, Vukans mannors helped twords this end as well she smiled and walked forward. She didnt speek but knelt to tilt his head up to her so he could see her as her hand came into view her wrist would be visable as the sleeve would fall back.

Scaring could be seen from where shackles had once been when he was looking at her she would smile and stand motioning for him to rise then bow in return making a sweeping jestur as if to say welcome and spoke tho with few words her voice was a soft it melodic and lovely sound. "Welcome Master Firelight an honor"

They visited for a time Wyn returning home to DruidOak so she could check on the others her crew taking shore leave and enjoying good food company music dancing and laughter.

Some fishing Rhannon came to visit checking on the ship she had built asking Wyn how she flew and was holding up between the realms.

Rhannon had gathered and distroyed all the chains that she could find with in each keep melting them down into nothing... as far as all knew none were left.

Wyn had let her know that she planned to reuturn to earth stopping by storms realm on the way to take the crystal fire and Stroms wine to earth..

....

Days later Rhannon on her way home from one of the mineing tunnels received an s.o.s signal from Honnora and changed corse heading for the ice caverns..

Honnora waited outside the ice caves entrance for rhannon to arrive she knew she would be along shortly.. tho honnora hated waiting she knew she couldnt take on this many demons on her own..

in addition one of the boys had gone missing.. the youngest.. Raiden had taken them fishing and the youngest Charrick, had gone into the bushes to take a leak and not come back.. Honora had tracked his scent here leaving the others to watch over Whiteoak.Honnora paced waiting.

Rhannon glided down landing in the snow not far from Honnora she could see there was more going on than she knew..from Honoras face. " what is it ? " as she approched Rhannon recgonized the scent of the younger boy stronger than it should be .. and nodded to Honnora she need not say anything at all.. drawing her blades she said. " lets go.."

Honora could see an alter and a few smaller demons imps circling a cage Charrick's crys could be heard coming from inside of it .. Honnora nodded sliently to Rhannon and took aim notching two arrows into her bow string.

stepping out into the open and firing pinning the two littler demons to the wall of the ice cave there body's struggling as they screached with pain dieing slowly.

Rhannon blades drawn as Honora pinned the two little ones to the wall rushed forward the two demons infront of her looking confused wondering which way to go one stayed to face Rhannon as she came at them the other headed for Honnora.

Honnora let lose another arrow lodging it in the demon advancing on her's sholder before swiftly loosing the bow string on her bow as the demon rushed her using the string like a whip the shaft of the bow held in both hands.

she wrapped the string around the demons neck and jerked hard enough with his speed to throw him off balance to the ground or break his neck.. she drew her dagger as the demon fell moving forward quickly intending to make sure of the kill.

she hadnt broken its neck however but had knocked it down the other demons scents were drawing stronger soon they would have more to deal with..she knew they had to have heard the squeels of the littler demons.

Rhannon's blades blocked the demon she faced's blow her swords catching his crossed in an x shape as she forced the demons larger heaver blade up and away from her.

spinning into the demon one sword aimed to impail it. The other comming across to slice its throat..a third demon rushing over had been to far away to aid at first was comming at Rhannons back.

Honnora reched the demon she had knocked downs side brining her dagger down to embed it in its throat when the demon brought its sword arm up in a wild swing to get her to back away from him so he could gain his feet.

Honnora did jump back ducking to avoid the wild swing and drew her other dagger at the same time the demon got to its feet the bow string still wrapped around its neck the string embedded enough in the skin that it had cut it and was bleeding.

Honnora still made no sound as she faced the demon the shaft of the bow still attatched to the string. she could hear the little one crying still in the cage.. the demon widened its stance..

Honnora grinned a very wicked looking grin as she rushed forward sliding between the demons legs grabbing hold of the bow shaft as she went intending to jerk the demon from its feet again.. the demon bringing his sword quickly downard intending to cut her down as she slid between his legs its wepon missing its mark.

Rhannon finnsihed off the first demon she had been facing not only with her own blades but by leaning and ducking to the side as the demon that had been coming up behind her brought his sword down in a powerful heavy down ward strike but rather than hitting her hit his fellow demon instead.

Rhannon grinned and brought her foot up pushing off of the now dead demon bringing her swords with her turning to now face the other demon who was pulling his sword from the other demons fleash.

Charrick screamed smelling death he was sure he was gonna die but he wasnt going down with out some fight and for all his little 5 yr old form could muster he took up the defrensive stance Honnora had tougth him and tryed to hit the demon who opened the cage door.

Honnora had mannagd to slip past the demon between his legs but wasnt quick enough to get to her feet to jerk him down before he turned bringing his blade up to strike however. He wasnt smart enough to have turned around fully and was attempting to hit her by only moving the upper half of his body.

which made him even more off balance, which still left Honnora between his legs. she used one of her daggers to stab the demons leg causing him to pause in his down ward strike howling with pain.

Rhannon facing the demon saw another heading for the cage with Charrick inside knew she would have to move swiftly. she heard the demon Honnora was fighing scream in pain but had her own to face she didnt dare take her gaze from her opponant..

The demon advanced coming at her swinging his sword in an up wards stroke from her lower left to her upper right Rhannon blocked the blow with one blade holding the sword up off of her.

Her arm num from the force of the blow as it vibrated down her arm she didnt drop her sword however, and brought her other around catching the demon in the sholder rather than the neck as she had inteneded.

she cut him and he backed off circling her .. Rhannon kept him in sight worrie for the boys safety had made her aim off she needed to focus dead they could do nothing for him.

Honnora while the demon was howling over his leg moved out from under him and quickly slit its throat she looked over to the cage hearing the boys scream silenced she feared the worst.. she pulled her blades from the demon.

Honnoras attention went to Rhannnon for a moment Rhannon seemed to be holding her own.. but from her angle it was hard to tell..

Honnora moved twords the youngling.. speaking for the first time .. her voice soft quiet and melodic but easly heard. " let the boy go.." her daggers were in hand she watched him closely seeing how he held the boy watching looking for a vunrable spot as the demon used the boy as a sheild.

Rhannon was struggling a bit this one was a little faster and stronger than the other had been and indeed the little ones crys along with the sounds of fighting had drawn two others from further back in the caves.

They needed to get out of there and to safety.. Rhannon moved forward to engage the demon only to have her attacks blocked. she backed off to try again her green eyes glittred in the darknes reflecting the light that emerged when she gathered energy to her and created flames in her hands.

Those flames spread down her swords the demon covered his eyes blinded momentarly giving Rhannon the advantage she needed she ducked under the demons blade as he swung wildly bringing one burning sword slicing across his belly.

while stepping past him as he fell she turned facing it pearcing him threw the back as he lay there to insure the demons death.

she looked up in time to see Honnora throw one of her daggers imbedding it in the eye socket of the demon holding Charrick. Rhannon ran over reaching them as the demon tossed the boy thowing him at Honnora in a rage and in an attempt to knock her down or distract her so it could flee.

Rhannon was already there waiting sword up as the demon turned it impailed itself on to her sword.." Honnora hurry we must go there are more on the way.. !"

Honnora nodded scooping up young Charrick in her hands and following Rhannon from the Ice caves.. as swiftly as possable the boy clinging to her the entire way.

....

Rhannon and Honnora took Charrick back to BelleRock as it was the closest Aden was teaching Sheara, Meela and Tela how to help cook and clean in the kitchen Braden Terrock Kara and Jaden were sparing with wooden swords in the court yard with sevral others as snow started falling.

it did often this far north in the mountins as they were Rhannon held the door open for Honnora as she carried the boy inside and asked Aden to bring soup a blanket and some Mulled wine for Honnora and herself.

She lead Honnora threw the court yard where the others practiced to one of the extra chambers Honnora lay Charrick down and looked him over aside from being quite shaken the boy was fine.

Rhannon accepted the soup and blanket from Aden as he brought them and handed them to Honnora stepping out as Honnora covered the boy and begain to feed him she walked with Aden back across the court yard.

Calling thos practicing to come inside and get ready as supper was about to start she motioned Aden into the library and spoke with him about what they had discovered in the ice cave.

Some demons had escaped the retaking of Easur and were making there homes in the ice caves and likely other mountin tunnels she and Aden would take turns at watch she contacted Riaden at WhiteOak to assure him Honnora and Charrick were fine safe and sound at BelleRock for the night and would return home in the morning.

she let him know what had been discovered as well and that Honnora was seeing to Charrick.. after that she contacted the other heads of house such as AuneAfae DragonBane, Donovan Firelight, Adewen DragonBorn, Wynwillow Druidoak requesting that they have a coucil meeting to discuss what she and Honnora had discovered and what then to do about it.

once finnished she rejoined the others at table all counting herself was present Aden, Terrock, the twins Jaden and Braden, Tela, Kara Sheara Meela and herself..on and on Aden told her he took a second bowl of soup to Honnora as she didnt wish to leave the boy.

Rhannon thanked him and asked after the day seeing how things went what each had learned and been practicing after supper had finnished she helped with there baths and to get them tucked into bed she got the idea then to make necklces for each family branch and soon made her way down to her work room to begin making molds for forgeing the jewlery. Occasionally checking on Charrick and Honnora.

Once the boy was safely back at WhiteOak and Honnora ready a council meeting was called. The only member not present at this council meeting was Wyn for she had taken a shipment run.

Honnora of the WhiteOaks, Donovan of the FireLights, Adewen of the DragonBorns, AuneAfae of the DragonBanes, and Rhannon of the BelleRocks were in attendance.

They met at the council grounds an open area with celtic like circular area with a small squair plat form mountins off in the distance to one side a river flowing round it in the other.

Each greeting the others formally as they arrived one by one before taking up ther positions around the circled area Rhannon rising after all had gathered and begain telling of what she and Honnora had discovered in the ice caves.. opening the discussion as to what was to be done about it.

Chapter 4

Elsewhere in another realm far away, a land where Dragons and Wyrms origonally came from. The elder dragons traveling through demensions as there own realm became croweded.

They spread out seeking other homes some to Earth, MaticRa a realm where beings that appeared Elven like tho not Elves were from and much more.

the Demon Realms they observed judging unworthy, or uninhabitable to there tastes moved on to others attacking the Demons they came across who invaded there lands taking there eggs to raise the hatchlings as servents or for other purposes.

Greystones arrival had come at an unfortunate time for tho he had come seeking to make a treaty they had never seen one such as he before and certinly never heard of a Damarian or the relm he claimed to come from called Easur.

He arrived not long after a raid by other Demons upon one of there Hatchery's, and so with out much question was imprisoned taken for one of the demons who had been apart of the raid.

They assumed left behind and trying to trick them by claiming he was a good being. To there minds he looked like a demon smelled like a demon and there for was a demon after all who had ever heard of a good one ?.

Some of the Dragons could take on human form not many of them, but a few and it was thos who mingled with another race of there realm beings they called Florianann's.

Plant like beings there main form of defense a poisonous pollin they produced or secreted depending on the Florianann they had other methods of protection as well and also acted as servents and spys working with the dragons in return for there protection and not burning there sections of the realm.

The Florianann's veried in green and blue hues from light to dark or verious combinations there of, some having purple pink and blue which also veryed in shades, there eyes were large lumanecent in yellow red and vivid blues.

However when they went into defense mode they changed from looking like live thriving plants to apearing like dead or dieing brown's and black as the poisions rose up threw there systems for them to weild.

Greystone Dragonborn had been sent to this acurssed realm he didnt know how long ago now, to observe and dissucss a possable treaty instead he had been imprisoned.

Bound with what he knew not save that it wasnt made from any miniral, or ore nor made of earth or clay. Something the plant like beings had made something about them and what they had done nullifyed his own abilitys with earth.

He was lowered into the ground and left to rot save when they rememberd to drop food or water to him ..ohhh how he longed for freedom and the chance to escape his captors to return home. he didnt understand ether why his kin had not come to free him from this.

He knew not nor did he know how long he was there for he had lost track of the days, had the demons attacked there home land had the others who had been sent out found alliances. Had they won or lost he had no way to know.

ohhh if he ever got free.. he wanted to take vengance, but tho he had understood why they had mistook him for the others and doing so might prove to there minds he was a demon as they thought and not good he hadnt been allowed to prove any different ether, and now how he hated Dragons.

Greystone's purple and blue eyes could see no light save for what filtered threw the whole above.. his wrists and akles were scared from having worn what ever bound him for so long..

He thought he was immagining things as a shape began to form in the shadows a female one at that. He knew he had finnally snapped, he had to have he didnt speak to it not yet.

shaking his head back and forth as he could swear she was speaking to him. He listened to the voice of the Damarian he was seeing telling him that things were going to be alright that she was going to help him escape and relased him from his bounds.

He had dreamed of escape so many times hoped for his people to find him and hated them for not coming for seemingly to have forgotten him. He thought he had was hallucinating.

Until she helped him bring his arms round infront of him which hurt like hell for he was stiff from being stuck in that position for so long the pain plus the water she gave him from a wine skin helped rouse him enough to make him aware that this really was happining. " Who ?"

She placed a finger against his lips " shuhh time enough to answer questions once were free of here. can you move ? " He slowly took another drink from the wine skin testing his limbs moving them slowly now he was unbound and could feel the energy of the earth around him.

He had the energy and the will but was weak yet and shook his head that he could not yet stand. She in turn asked his permission to heal him for which he nodded his acceptance of her offer. He still dared to wonder if this was all in his mind and didnot speak further as of yet.

she worked quickly and healed what she could with out draining her own energy too much and together they escaped, they didnt go which ever way she had come in, for she explained that she was still mastering her skills and tho she could come and go she could not yet take another with her.

instead he used his earth abilitys to open a tunnle in the pit from where he had been placed traveling below ground until they were well away from the area much like a rabbit or ground hog hole on a larger scale they emerged.

Grey had many questions how had she gotten past the dragons and found him who was she what of the plant like beings and so on.

Now he could see her more clearly he could tell she was a Firelight, and quite young only just past the introduction ceremony age perhaps younger yet. He didnt recognize her only her coloring giving him a clue as to which family branch or clan she belonged to. " Hurry weve not much time i'll take you to"

before she could say more her body jerked and her eyes widened he reached out in time to catch her an arrow potruded from her back. he ducked as another flew past his head.

He lifted her in his arms and took off into the surrounding area the damn able trouble with that was thos plant like beings blended in so well with the reagon there was no way to tell them from the actual plant life.

"r.. right.. p..po..ket.. cry.. crystal.." Greystone looked down at her as he contined to run " dont talk" was all he said his voice a deep base cracking and harsh sounding from disuse. As he kept going he had no idea where to go and the female in his arms breathing was becoming laybored.

Any time he thought he might have lost them another arrow would sound and hit one of the trees his own element usless against them. Over head could be heard Dragons roaring in the distance as they too had been made aware of the escape and joined the hunt.

Grey cursed and slid to a hault drawing up the earth creating a cave like structure around them buying them just enough time. He broke the arrow off laying her on her side.

He got the crystal from her pocket.." hold on dont give up on me yet ill get us to safety and get you healed " Useing the crystal he teleported himself and the female to Easur.

They arrived on the broken steps of the castle that had been reduced to rubble. As it was he didnt notice his surroundings yet. However as he immediately reached for the female who had freed him to grant her aid as she had done for him.

To find that what ever poision the plant like beings had used was fast acting on there kind, and the female had died. Had he been able to stop and heal her right away she might have lived but there had not been time.

Greystone DragonBorn held the female in his arms and cryed for he hadnt even known her name her people would know tho and he would return her body to them.

Looking up at his surroundings for the first time the greif he felt for the female turned to shock and anger as he registered the ruines before him.

He got to his feet not even remembring doing so as he looked around. What had happened here to this once proud castle and place of council where were the Damarians more questions and no answers.

He was unaware he had moved walking around the ruins he could see they were sevral years old moss vines and small trees were growing up around them however in the center was a statue where stones had been cleared away so it stood alone.

He moved closer he could see the statue was of his niece Idrialla. Tho she was dressed differently then he had ever seen her and appeared to be armed, when he had seen her last she had been nothing but a healer and midwife.

Below the statue was a plaque that read. Our saviour Idrialla DragonBorn May her Courage Continue As Example To Us All. Apparently what ever had happened his niece had played a large part in the battling why then had the castle not been rebuilt he wondered.

Turning back to where he had left the girls body he gathered her once more in his arms and took to the air flying twords Firelight Keep, and Village. His movements and flight were slow jerky and he hurt from head to toe his joints popped on occasion.

However he was determined. Arriving at Firelight keep he was further stunned to see that that keep was distroyed in verious stages of repair had him turning to the village near at hand.

It was where he met with Donovan the head of Firelight house now and thos there explaining all that had happened he found out the Firelight who had saved him's name had been Ashwyn.

She had been young Damarian who had been apart of the female he had loved Ember's family and had heard tales of her older sister being sent out with Greystone and others to different realms and gone seeking answers. Sadly she had never found Ember in her wonderings but had found Greystone.

Donovan further explained that the reason she had been able to get past the Dragons and plants undetected was because her element's were rare ones that few still around them weilded.

That of darkness and silence, but not as developed as they might have been for she could move undetected on her own but couldnt quite take another with her with out being seen.

Grey thanked Donovan for his time as well as for the name of the female that had saved him leaving he went to DragonBorn Keep where he would confront his great neice the half breed Adewen, and challange her for head of House.

Adewen stood on the ramparts of DragonBorn keep looking up at the night sky there was no moon this night but the stars shown bright twinkling in the inky blueish black ness that was there background.

Lost in her own thoughts she almost didnt know that Wolfen had joined her to look across the fields below it was a quite night and all seemed well. "Gem for your thoughts ? tho i know there worth much more"

At his words she turned her silvery gaze upon him. a gentle smile formed. "i was thinking about the past, and my mother, remembering some of our training sessions at the training grounds on earth. Of all her hopes and goals for the future. I sometimes wonder if shed be pleased with all we have done".

Before Wolfen could answer a Damarian they had never seen before a DragonBorn by his coloring landed before them and called out a challange for head of house. Adewen could not refuse. " Wolfen protect idri should it be needed" Wolfen nodded and bowed leaving her to do as asked.

While away after having deliverd some cargo and goods to some friends of hers she had helped to seek safety from the teriny of a bad ruler, she had almost forged an alliance with, but upon discovering the true neture of the kingdom involved she had helpled free the people instead.

Wyn was able to help those who had need of it, a vaga bond loyal group of friends of all types a lycon who was there leader Aria, a shifter who took on dragon form, by the name of Meralian, as well as Adewens friend Cobra who resided among them. Iconiclast or Icon for short had become Wyns main first mate aboard ship.

Before leaving earth Wynwillow was invited to meet with there good friend Devon where upon she was asked to perforom his and Destinys wedding ceremony.. she agreed happily to do so for them and was introduced to the bride.

She was dressed in her ushual attire but given another garment to wear once she agreed to performe the ceremony.

"Love this is Lady WynWillow DruidOak of the Damarian clan of Easur, Wyn, Destiny.. She agreed to Wed us love. "He said going to Desitnys side kissing her gently on the lips before stepping back to allow Wyn closer.

Wyn bowed and waited until Devon gave her room before stepping forward a friendly smile upon her features as she spoke "An honor ta meet ye miss an ta be asked ta do this fer ye both."

Destiny smiled and looked at Wyn curiouly she had seen only one other damarin before and that long ago before she died that had been Idrialla.

Wyn was somewhat different her coloring was a light bue black and white, and her eyes a beautiful pink coloring that was very intrueging.." Hello Wyn. its nice to meet you as well. Sorry about the short notice."

Devon gently took his loves hand as he spoke obviously having forgotten hed already spoken with her about the damarians and thos he was connected with she just hadnt met them yet. "Wyn isnt from around here......She's Damarian"

Destiny smiles up at her soon to be husbend as he took her hand and asked. " Then she knows Idri ?"

Devon nods to her answering " She does they are family"

Wynwillow gently interjected "no exactly family but aye close same clan an race.. warms me heart ta see Idri be remembered among ye. Tho she no longer be wi us now. " she smiles continuing.

"Adewen, Idrialla's daughter would ha come wi me, but she recently had twins an sad ta say lost one o them.. hower well no speak on such as of now this be a happy time fer ye an thos ye love.."

Destiny looked concerned for the woman she hadnt yet met Please. " if you need anything, let me know."

Changing the subject Devon spoke. " Wyn, thank you for doing this"

Wynwillow nodded in understanding being poilite and respectful she could be diplomatic when necessary just 90 persent of the time she chose not to. " yer welcome allow me ta change an take me place then we may begin."

Devon chuckled thinking it would be the first time and most likely the last time he would see Wynwillow in a dress. " of course"

"och an i almost fergot, may i invite another ta join as well? he be no far away just on me ship" Wyn wasnt sure why she thought Vukan might wish to attend the wedding but it wasnt often they got to observe things such as this and she knew she couldnt invite her whole crew but ..

"mmhmm.." Devon looked thoughtful as Destiny replyed " Of Course"

"thank ye " wyn stepped off to the side to use her crystal to invite Vukan to join her. he had found his sister traveling around, and they had, had a very happy and loving reunion telling each other of there ventures and all that had happened sense they had been seperated.

Laila continued her travels introducing her brother to Vaul the pride demon who also had met up with Laila in her travels. The two had fallen in love or so it seemed they did very well together.

Vukan very rarely ever left his sisters side wanting to make up for lost time, hardly ever did you now see one with out the other, but this time Laila had gone to Easur to meet with Donovan and the other Firelights that had survived she would meet up with her brother later.

Destiny gazes over at another woman standing not far away and points to Luna a friend of her's wings. wispering softly as she admired them "So beautiful."

Devon gazed at his bride with love and hope for the future before looking back at Wyn saying " everyone's gettign ready best you do so as well"

Wynwillow removes her wepons handing them to Devon " i trust ye ha a safe place ta stash these till tis oer ?"

Devon StormBringer hands them back, peace knotting them" that works " Wyn looked at him but still stashed them she wasnt worried about hurting anyone but thought it might look odd for the one performing the wedding to be armed to the teeth, and so stashed them in the back out of the way hoping they would be safe enough

The gown Wyn changed into was a black gown with a see threw white gausy material in a toga style over the left sholder pinned with a celtic gold emblem at the left sholder leaving the right bare. Belted with a gold celtic linked belt under the breasts to hold it in place.

Shifting to human form took her long hair that had been up in a high ponytail and shook it loose brushing it and then braiding it in to two smaller brades on ether side of her head joining the two in the middle.

Forming them into one brade down the rest of her back, her skin was a creamy white coloring combine with her pink colored eyes and pointed ears she looked like something out of a fiary tale or dream.

Devon paces nervously at the altar pausing when Wyn comes out suprised tho he knew he shouldnt be and shook his head smiling greatfully that his friend was willing to do this for him.

Wynwillow bows politely taking her place at the alter, and smiles reasuringly " twill be aright yell see"

Destiny takes in a deep breath before she walks over to the side so she can change. She was worried that she was going to trip, or that something bad would happen.

She was very shakey at this moment from all the nerves. She didn't sleep much from the excitement rushing through her head. She knew that today was a beautiful day. She wondered how everyone else was doing out there in the main room.

Devon took a breath did his best to remain calm " Neko....come with me buddy, you get to stand up here with Grampa"

Wynwillow was nervous herself but she knew no where near as nervous as the bride and groom and had a feeling. one day she would be just as nervous that is if she ever found the courage to say yes to merrage.

funny she thought she could face invaders dragons and giants as well as other demons but the thought of wedding made her nervous as hell.. however this day was about there friend and Devon the damarians ally and his soon to be bride a wonderful woman to be sure.

Devon continued speaking with Neko "over here ..behind me.. Thats it"

"Do ye both ha yer own vows when it be time ?" Wyn asked wondering if she would needs do that part as well or not.

"we do" Devon replyed looking nervous again.

Wyn smiles softly noding

Luna Valerian takes Chaos's hand and smiles up to him. " Reay love? " she would raise up on her tiptoes and kiss his forehead. " You going to be ok to make your walk? " giggling softly, she would lay her head on his as it rested on her shoulder, he was still recovering from his wounds and was tired.

Devon decided to remind Neko of his very important task. " neko buddy, when this pretty lady asks for the rings, yo can give them to us, ok?"

Neko nods in agreement not speaking.

Wynwillow gives Devon a look when he calls her pretty but makes no comment looking to little Neko. "an honor ta meet ye lad i be Wynwillow "offers hand in friendship.

Devon smiles feeling a little less nervous talking about Neko " this is my grandson neko, a knight in training too"

Luna Valerian kisses Chaos again and walks over to Destiny to see if she needs any help changing and to help straighten her dress and veil last minute

Neko looks up at Wyn and edges closer to his grandpa " hello"

Devon StormBringer looks an antique watch he has in his pocket, almost looking like the white rabbit," lords, we are running late."

Destiny giggles softly seeing Luna coming over to help her. She knew that it was going to be a long day. She knew that the time was flying by and things were already late.

Places her left hand under Luna's chin still holding on to the bright smiles." I am fine, Luna. Just my nerves are getting to me at this moment. Does everything look okay around here? " There was worry in her eyes.

Wynwillow closes her eyes a moment she hadnt seen Vukan enter as of yet tho he had said he would join her.

Devon looks down the Aisle nervously. Wyn opened her eyes and seeing him said " breath me friend"

Devon smiled softly at Wyns encoragement seeing she looked a little nervous herself tho if one didnt know her well you never would have guessed and he had to chuckle a bit thinking shed be far more comfortable as a goomsman. " I'm fine.....I just want to day to be perfect for her"

Wynwillow nodded in agreement "twill be"

Neko stood waiting with the rings he was a 5yr old lycon youngling doing his best to stand still shifting from foot to foot and playing with the lacings on the pillow he held with the rings attatched. Devon looking down to Neko, smiling.

Wynwillow continued attempting to be reasuring " How could it no en were it just the two o ye present tis about tha two o ye becomin one wether the rest o us be present er no"

Luna Valerian smiling soft and warmly at Destiany " No absolutely not, everything is a mess " she says in a voice caught some where between deadly serroius and trying not to laugh, running her thumb under Destiny's eyes to clear up the slight smudged liner. " You look beautiful and everything is perfect, no need to worry"

Destiny Couldn't help but laugh at her friend's joke. She knew that things were in their place, She stands on her tippy toes and whispers up in to Luna's ear. "Thank you for being here. Please, go help Chaos, and I am ready when you are."

She lowers herself down with that smile on her face. Placing her hands together on to her flowers. She was ready to get this ball rolling.

Chaos Holding onto Lunas hand he lowered his head a bit and smiled at his love, he was happy to be able to be here and have the most wonderful woman at his side through it.

"I'll be alright for a short walk.... i hope. " Keeping his balance he watched Luna walk off and held his side, he wasn't going to move until he had to and hoped that his health wasn't a issue for his family. " A long as i can have a helping hand i will make it through the day."

Looking around at the room he smiles softly and fidgited with his tie a bit, he might have been the more intellectual of the souls but he still did not like a suit, his smile broadened further when his Luna returned to him a short while later.

Wynwillow spoke out to the room in genral " be there others were waitin on afor we start ?"

Devon answered " we are good we should get started"

Wynwillow asked again " do ye ha any music ye wish ta play ?"

Devon again answered " no, due to some folks " he continues glancing down the Aisle unable to help himself his hands were shaking so he closed them into fists to help hide that fact.

Wynwillow smiles and nods watching down the aisle fer the bride.

Luna smiling warmly, and leaning in to lightly kiss Choas cheek she helped him into position then took up her own.

Devon smiles, as he nods to them, his face showing alot of nerves.

....

Destiny slowly comes out from the back and looks around. Taking in a deep breath just before she makes her way in to the main room. She holds her head up and grips on to the flowers.

"Breath...breath...breath.... " She blows out quickly. Stepping out to the runner. She holds her head up high slowly walking down the aisle. Looking forward trying to hold back her tears.

Devon smiles, watching her approach, as he reaches up, brushing away something from his cheek.

All eyes were on the bride she was a beautiful sight with her long flowing gown and vail. Wynwillow smiles as the bride begins to make her way twords them, and mentaly begins prepairing what she will say.

Vukan entered the room just in time for the wedding to begin glad he hadnt missed anything yet and also glad Wyn had sent for him. He was pleased she rememberd him tho he was sad to hear of Adewens loss.

He knew as did the others she would recover and take joy in her remaining youngling he hopes they will forgive his attire as he had arrived a little late and stood in the back so as not to interupt.

Destiny pauses at the bottom of the stairs looking up at everyone with a smile on her face. Holding his hand lightly she was shining. She holds a bit of her skirt up as she makes it up the stairs.

She smooths out her skirt as she makes it up to alter. She smiles more waving at Luna and Chaos. She waves at Neko on the other side of Devon. She mumbles." I love you...you ready for this?"

Devon nods, as he smiles like a fool unable to speak for the moment.

Wynwillow's attention was on the bride and groom as well as the ceremony about to take place. She reconginzed Vuken's scent and was glad he had been able to make it. Smiling as she watched Devon go to help his bride the rest of the way up the isle.

Upon rejoining her where she stood with the others present she began doing her best to keep her accent from coming forth so that thos present could understand her better.

"Love is the reason we are here. In marriage we not only say, I love you today, but also, I promise to love you for all of our tomorrows."

"Devon and Destiny in the days ahead of you, there will be stormy times and good times, times of conflict and times of joy. I ask you to remember this advice."

Chaos Gripping Lunas hand he smiled and kissed her lips softly he felt a bit silly but it was best he sat for the ceremony, his eyes looking down the isle at Destiny.

he'd made it a point to be here for his siblings and he was. Bowing his head to Destiny as she got to the alter he didn't say a word however and sighed a releved sound.

Vukan watches all sensing the happy nervousness of those joining together. He sticks to the background having barely made it.

Wynwillow's voice continued Vukan leaned against the wall listining a slow smile touching his lips feeling pride in his friend.

"Never go to bed angry...Let your love be stronger than your anger... Learn the wisdom of compromise, for it is better to bend than to break."

"Believe the best of your beloved rather than the worst... Confide in your partner and ask for help when you need it....Remember that true friendship is the basis for any lasting relationship...Give your spouse the same courtesies and kindnesses you bestow on your friends....Say I love you every day."

"i believe a this time the bride an groom ha written there own vows.. if ye would per seed pls " she smiles glad shed managed to speak clearly for the most part unable to help the slip as she relaxed.

Devon took his loves hands in his and looked at her has he spoke " Destiny....You have been walking behind me for 5 years, watching me, protecting me. you have always been there, and I was a fool for not seeing it. but on today, this Day...OUR day."

"I want you to walk beside me, as my friend, my lover and most importantly as my Wife. we will face challenges, of all sizes and types, but with each other, we will overcome them, no matter what. we have Our family, Each other, Children, grand Children, and Friends."

Destiny tears up but holds them in...well trying to at least. She smiled hearing his vows. They were very sweet. She nods squezing his hand lightly, beginning her own vows. " Devon, my love, my heart, you are the prince that girls dream of. You are the knight in shining armor that always is there to help those in danger."

"I love that about you. I love your mind, how you always care about those around. I promise to look after you to protect you and to grow old with you. In good times and in bad, you are beside me to help guide me. I know that together we can take on every task. I am blessed to have you in my life. You have shown me that there is true love out there, and with me, its you."

Wynwillow pauses a few moments letting there words and the meanings behind them be taken in by all then asks- The rings pls.. - she smiles at little Neko turning to him.

Devon smiles, looking at Neko " pst.....buddy, yer on" Wyn asked again " lad ? the rings pls chuckling at Nekos nervousness Devon, picks the rings up, nodding to proceed.

Wynwillow smiles and nods as the groom gets the rings " The ring, an unbroken, never ending circle, is a symbol of committed, unending love. Devon, as you place this ring on Destiny's finger, repeat these words after me."

she paused giving him a bit of time before continuing " This ring, a gift for you, symbolizes my desire that you be my wife from this day forward. As this ring has no end neither shall my love for you."

Devon smiles, sliding the hand crafted Onyx ruby and diamond ring upon her finger" This ring, a gift for you, symbolizes my desire that you be my wife from this day forward. As this ring has no end neither shall my love for you."

Wynwillow spoke to Destiny next. " Destiny as you place this ring on Devon's finger, repeat these words after me " Wyn smiles at both bride and groom.

"This ring, a gift for you, symbolizes my desire that you be my husband from this day forward. As this ring has no end neither shall my love for you"

Destiny smiles looking at his hand with the ring. Feeling the ring slide up her finger. She looks over at Luna.

"Devon chuckles, as he places the ring she is to use in her hand and whispers- I took the liberty of helping" Luna smiles and remains silent

Destiny takes the ring sliding it slowly on to his ring finger " This ring, a gift for you, symbolizes my desire that you be my husband from this day forward. As this ring has no end neither shall my love for you."

"Devon and Destiny, in your journey of life together, remind yourselves often of the love that brought you together. Give the highest priority to your love. When challenges come.

"Remember to focus on what is right between you. In this way, you can ride out the storms. And when clouds hide the sun in your lives. Remember, even if you lose sight of it for a moment, the sun is always there."

"Devon and Destiny you have committed yourselves to each other in marriage by the exchanging of vows, and by the giving of rings."

"With the authority vested in me as head o the DruidOak family branch o Easur an Damarian Clan reperesentitive, with great joy, I now pronounce ye husband and wife...... May you live together in blissful happiness from this day forward. YOU MAY SEAL YOUR VOWS WITH A KISS!"

Devon smiles at Wyns words, pulling Destiny close as he kisses her deeply, and lovingly.

Wynwillow shook her head smiling speaking to them and thos present " with the autortity vested in me as Head of Druidoak house i now pernounce ye Mr. an Mrs. StormBringer"

Destiny kisses him back happily, bairly aware of what Wyn was saying or the others around them until a short time after the kiss ended and Devon motions to Neko to comeover for a big hug, and looking out at his friends saying " thank you, all of you"

Luna Valerian claps happily and smiles warmly, leaning down to kiss Chaos's cheek.

Wynwillow nods saying " yer most welcome congradulations to ye both"

Devon held Destiny in his arms Neko stood near his side " I know its been a rough Journey, but you all have been there every step of the way"

Luna wiped a way happy tears as she said " Congradulations, may you be blessed"

Wyn wispered "blessed be ta ye both"

Destiny recovering herself blushed saying " Yes, thank you all for coming. And enjoying this moment with us."

Vukan had been Watching the service and Wyn's amazing way of holding herself up during a beautiful ceremony. A small tear of joy wells up as he sees her in a new light. He stepped forward as well " Congratulations to both of you"

Devon nodded knowing he must be the one Wyn had invited to join them " we would like you to stay and enjoy our hospitality, thank you for coming"

Destiny nods her head to the man." Thank you for letting us borrow her. She is a wonderful person."

Devon grins " my wife.....and yes, ive been dying to say that.....has worked hard to provide a place to relax"

Wynwillow smiles and looks around only now letting any of her nervousness show but only somone looking closely would notice. she saw Vukan in the back and moved to join him Wyn wasnt one to wear dresses but she was happy to have helped the couple.

Chaos opening his eyes he looked over to the new bride and groom, his eyes holding a shine before he turns his head just in time to steal a kiss form Luna and grins." You're welcome my old friend, may ... whatever you want come true... brain isn't working...."

Vukan found Wyns wepons in the back and picked them up knowing she would want them and waited for her to join him " would you like to change and get out of here ?"

Wyn grins hearing that kisses him on the cheek before saying " Gladly where did ye stash me wepons ? " she had seen him gather them from the back as he had waited for her.

Devon chuckles over hearing Wyns words. Destiny smiling next to him asking him why he was chuckling giggled as he leaned down to quietly answer her.

Luna Valerian would close her eyes and mumble something softly under her breath and then claps her hands, and confetti would rain from the raffters and burst into fizzing little sparkly lights to dance around the room.

Destiny reolizing Wyn was getting ready to change and go said "Please stay around so I can get some portrates of everyone. We have cake here and free boose at the tavern. We will like everyone to feel free to anything they want."

Devon looks at Vukan.. as he lets go of Destiny and moves with him slightly off to the side " Wyns a wonderful woman and friend .. " he was cut off from saying more as Wyn called out and both of them looked over at her.

"Blast means i canna change yet"

He grinned over Wyns words and spoke on a different line he would get back to Vukan later Wynwillow s a friend and he wouldnt see her hurt she was like a little sister to him hed known her for a very long time, but this was not the right time. " I would like to thank Chaos and Luna for all thier hard work. Neko for standing beside his silly grampa and beautiful Gramma"

Vukan understood what Devon was getting at with out him having to go into it any further saying if only to himself as Devon moved away

“ Yes that she is. “ Vukan smiles as he looks in her direction finding those beautiful pink eyes as she walks over and he answers her origonal question.

“No sword or bow yet my love your dress is gorgeous on you, however here are your daggers” he hands them to her.

Wynwillow looked at him greatfully as he handed them to her “ ahh thank ye Vukan “ she slips her daggers on feeling instantly more at ease and much more comfortable the folds of the gown hidding them from view.

“i want everyone over here “ Hearing and seeing the excange between Wynwillow and Vukan Devon smiled knowing Vukan had taken his meaning and that he wouldnt hurt her. Wyn he knew could care for herself in many ways. She as well as his other damarian friends and allies deserved to be happy as well and if he could help in any way he would.

Wynwillow looked at Vukan then back at Devon and the others moving to join them “ just let me know when an where ye want me”

Devon’s eyes glittered with humor he couldnt help himself as he said “ I am sure that can be arranged” Luna Valerian blushes at what she hears

Wynwillow glared at him and then smiled almost evily “ ye do know i ken still take ye down dress er no right”

Luna Valerian called out to change the subject before it got too out of hand “ ON TO THE RECEPTION!!!”

Wolfen entered he was Devons adopted brother an ancent dragon who could take on human form he had just come from speaking with Lady Adewen of the DragonBorns he is little idri’s Guardian when she is away on earth or at council.

Adewen had spoken to the council on his and other dragons behalfs who wanted to escape earth and the human hunters among other beings who wished to use them for there own purposes to do something in return for the deed she had done for them.

Wynwillow recognizing Wolfen moved to speak with him " Greetns Wolfen tis good ta see ye again"

Wolfen Chuckles "Its good to see you Wyn.." she smiled " Aye indeed me frien tis vera good ta see ye.. be wee idri gettin stronger ? " she asked.

Wolfen nodded that indeed she was then moved on to greet his brother and new sister. Wyn moves closer to Vukan sliding her arm around his waist watching the goings on quietly.

"Your words were well said and with such meaning. is that how you would like to follow as well?" Vukan asked her happy to have her back at his side. He wondered at her thoughts on such matters.

Wyn looked back at Vukan a suprised and thoughtful expreassion to her features she was speechless for the moment and blushed and was saved from answering right away being called over for portrates and moved to stand as directed.

Wyn walks back over to Vukan when allowed a break. Her thoughts having been on his question did she wish to wed to be Vukans wife in the humans way as well as his mate.. aye she did but was she ready at this time so much was happining in there lives and with the damarians in one fashion or another it ..

a few months ago Wyn knew her answer would have been no because she would have thought he was kidding and only teasing her, but the more she came to know him the more she found she liked, and was begining to see things and herself in a differnt light.

Before she couldnt have immagined she would ever have a mate and love let alone anything else and now... now she could honestly see a life of happiness with him however they hadnt known one another long and she still had to track down that crystal and distroy it or return it to Easur..

Vukan waits for them to get done listening to the joyful banter and love throughout the room As Wyn returns he sees she is in thought and smiles knowing he has caused her to think different lately. He is curious if she means it not to go to bed angry to always remember together we could can figure things out if we love and care for each other.

Wyn smiled up at Vukan as she reached him " Do ye mean what ye asked are ye askin ?" she wasnt aware of it but she was holding her breath waiting to hear his responce.

Vukan chuckles at her questions. " yes my love. i am asking if the ideals you spoke of is how you want us to live by? if you thought i was asking you to marry me not yet i would like to do a proper proposal and one with meaning! " He smiles as he puts an arm around her waist looking into her eyes.

Wynwillow let out the breath she was holding and nodded taking his hands in hers she looked over at the couple then back up to Vukan.

"aye indeed i do beleive in what i said. A fore i met ye i didna trust much o anyone. ye ken tha more than most, but with ye i feel anythin be possable no matter the chos we should take what er we can. An focus on the good no matter how fleetin it may be makes it all the mur preshous when it comes."

Luna hugged her friend and then stood next to her teasingly asking "Well Destiny, are you looking forward to the wedding night? And will little feet soon after be paddign around the tavern?"

Destiny smiles and blushes after returning her friends hug. " I am looking forwards to my wedding night, with my husband. Oh my gosh, I got married" she giggles. "And if Gaia blesses us with children, I would be the happiest woman on this planet."

Chaos chuckling softly he nips Lunas neck " I want little feet padding around out home... but i'm not well enough to make that so. " Looking away he sighed softly trying to make Luna change her mind on her decision he wasn't healthy enough, a smile on his lips however for Destiny.

Wyn hearing the conversation said " i dunna mean ta intrude bu.. we damarians ha a healin ability.. perhpas if ye would na mind me tryin i could aid ye"

Luna Valerian blushes and swats his rump lightly " You are very naughty, telling all these people what you been hinting and down right asking for, you should be ashamed for telling our private life to any who will listen " she tried to have a stern voice, but her eyes and big smile to her lips were easily read that she was laughing on the inside

Chaos Valerian Looking at the ground he didn't want to admit to someone he had just met that his health was going down hill rapidly, shaking his head he looked up to the woman and smiled innocently while pulling his wife closer to him." i am a bit unable to stand for a long period of time, i'm healing on my own so i'll be alright madam."

Looking to Destiny his eyes showing her that he wasn't teling the truth but he didn't want to speak on his truths." Luna has been tending to me as well as Devon when need be, but on that note.... can i get a pivate healing session with my beautiful nurse?"

"o corse apologies fer intrudin " bows politely " if ye should er wish fer me er en another o me kin ta try ye need only ask.. Devon ken reach us twould be an honor ta aid ye as ye are friend ta Devon an Destiny an threw them ours as well"

Vukan watched Wyn with a sense of pride and happiness as she caught his eye and since than she has been a blessing to him, he is grateful she feels that way. in a playful teasing voice Vukan pulled wyn back into his arms and asked " So you won't go to bed angry at me ever?"

Destiny where would ye like vukan an i ? " hearing his question she grins looking up at him. " nay ill yell at ye afor hand an get it all out by the time we get ta the bed nether o us will be angry i promise" “shall we go ?” i believe we should we have things that need to be attended to I am thinking. “ he winks and grabs her ass firmly while bending down to kiss her cheek. “ Would you like to say your goodbyes to all instead of just leaving suddenly, I mean you were the one to marry them my sweet.”

Wyn tilts her head nodding not giving away his action “aye indeed”

Luna Valerian smiles. “ Well I guess we should be going too “ she blushes and looks to Chaos

Wynwillow nodded to them “ i wish ye all a plesent eve an look forward ta seein ye again in future fer now i beleive well take our leave. an wish ye all the best “ she finds the rest of her wepons and changes back to her ushal attire.

Wynwillow moved back to Vukans side looking up at him as she asked “ ye ready fer this ?”

“i is “ he says he is tickled knowing she wants to fight and hunt not only that, but she had an amazing way about her of remaining light hearted enough to laugh tease and banter with out losing herself in the past a way of making thos around her smile and laugh.

Eventually she will find he enjoys such as well. lightning can be seen within his blue eyes. “With you at my side not sure if ready is correct, confident yes, reassured your with me yes, others be damned hell yes. I am going with YES. “ he laughs and chuckles as she walks as he reolizes she might not have heard all he had said for she had already started walking away after bowing to the others again.

Wynwillow bows plolitely to the others once more and turns striding out the doors her expression hidden as she relolized he had been calling her love this whole time. As well as nearly perposed.

The only problem was they hadnt known one another very long yet, but some how she felt as he apparently did that they belonged. However as she listened to his words while heading for the door she couldnt help grinning her heart felt light and full.

Vukan quickly catches up so they can get going mumbling to himself " damn she is an excitiing creature " there his words trail only into thoughts of how she is exciting to him.

when she gets serious about battle or the way her eyes alight when she laughs.. the way she walks and the way her... He remembers to follow before she can exit the doors he doesn't want to miss a moment of her smiling he strides to keep her in sight.

....

Vukan remained with Wyn for a few months before returning to join his sister Laila and Vaul who had invited him a few months before to join them, having had accepted the invitatin long ago couldnt back out now. Wynwillow was reluctent to see him go having grown very close to him.

She had not yet admited save to herself that she was falling in love. Before she told him she had to accomplish something she set out to do and tho she wishe d he could stay with her it would be harder to hide her actions.

so Wynwillow continued on with out him, she hugged and kissed him good by hopeing when or if she returned they might have a future.

Wynwillows ship the Orical set sail sail after leaving Vukan of the Firelight's on earth with his sister Laila and Vaul to work with Adewen's adopted sister Eva and her mate a group of earthly non humans.

a seperate group from the ones Wyn had helped. The Deamos group. They banded together to help fight off darker demons of earth to protect the humans and at the same time try to keep there activitys and so forth secret from human eyes.

Adewen's other sister Rina had assisted them from time to time but had been killed during one of the battles Adewen been unable to go to her sisters for aid. Idri being too young she had sent word to Wyn and Vukan asking if one of them could go in her stead. Vukan had accepted and met up with his sister and Vaul who had agreed to accompany him.

When he questioned Wynwillow on why she wasnt going as well she said only that she could not that there were other matters of equil importance she needed to attend to but would meet up with him again at a later date.

She also permoted Iconiclast.. her first mate and a Demon of another realm to captin of his own ship, and let him go his own way with the promise of aid to her should she ever require it. He had readly given his word. Wyn embraced him in a friendly hug patting him on the back as they christioned his new ship the Challanger.

ohhh that had been a wild night for the crew.. shore leave aplenty for all as well as a parting of good friends. Some of the crew joined with Icon. Wyn did not mind she had an idea what she was headed into. Sure icons strenght and skills would be of great use, however she couldot risk him.

....

Many days had passed sense then and she was looking over a copy of some maps on her desk in the captins cabin shed already marked off sevral spots and was still cursing the fact that Ade had seen her over looking the ones on Easur.

she hoped Adewen wouldnt put two and two together for awhile. Walking over to her cabinet she pulled out a bottle of rum and was turning round to walk back to her desk not having yet uncorked it a thought ful and frustrated expression on her features.

Shed checked sevral realms now with no luck save a few they didnt dare enter such as the dragons territory, and the elven realms.. she knew who ever had reached the large crystal before she could wouldnt go there eather .. to dangerous.. humm

The ship rocked back with the waves as it coarsed through the ocean heading steadfast towards it's distination. the canvas of the sails streched by some unfelt wind which pushed against them and the ship, the wake behind the ship cresting into six and seven foot waves as the ship itself moved almost impossibly fast for a sail driven vessel.

The lighting of the captains cabin was dim, the lanterns giving a faint slightly off white glow. and with a sudden burst the doors to the captain's cabin flung open the sight behind them no longer being of the ship the cabin was attached to but instead was a darkness which reached out to silence the light of the lanterns.

The sound of the darkness was that of a an electrical storm, and through the darkness stepped a dark form of a being. Only noticeable by the outline of purple light which showed it to obviously not be a Damarian.

The form of this creature from what could be seen was almost that of a man except for the large antlers which nearly scraped the frame of the door as he stepped inside the captain's cabin. Just as suddenly as the darkness appeared it was gone leaving this antlered dark skinned being standing in the captain's cabin.

Wyn was used to the sway and rock of the ship she smiled fondly as she looked at the bottle of rum in her hand remembering Storm of the novapaws challanging her to a drinking contest some months back, she chuckled as she remembered he had lasted alot longer than most and had almost.. almost won.. ahh good times.

Suddenly she tensed setting the bottle swiftly down upon the desk feeling the change in the air flow turning to face the doors as they burst open, dagger in hand to see a being she didnt recognize as from earth or any other realm she had been too.

Behind him a nothingness and darkness that streatched into nothing, an ability some damarians posessed as did other Demon types question was. Be this friend or foe.. raising her empty hand she used her own wind ablitys.

Her hand glowed with a soft sworling white light as the being stepped forward she released it. at first it appeared to be aimed directly at him but it devided before reaching him going round him to sweep the doors closed once more.

A heart beat after she released the energy manipulating the air she threw her dagger aiming not to kill but intending to aim for his sholder and pin him to the door seconds after it closes behind him..

She took up a defensive stance incase her actions failed prepaired to fight if necessary.." Who are ye ? an what are ye doin on me ship ? Who sent ye ? " Wyns pink colored eyes flashed as she demanded answers

The dagger knocked against his armoured pauldron and clattered to the deck harmlessly, the being raising its hands in surrender his expression going quickly from excitement to confusion as he clutched his shoulder feeling the nick her dagger had made in his shiney engraved feywooden armour.

"n no one sent me" he stampered out "I came of my own volition" he stumbled to the side as what he percieved as ground beneath him swayed with the waves. "what im doing is my own business" he stated as he lost his balance and tottered to the deck.

Wyn walked up to the being her eyes still glittering dangerously at his words but it was clear as he stumbled and fell that he was no sailor and there for tho it still remained to see if he were an enemy or not..

He had obviously not been sent by anyone who knew her any at all to attack els they would have chosen better and found a sailor of sorts. There was a hint of humor in her eyes and the half slight smile that touched her lips as she approched she grabbed his arm and haulled him to his feet.

Steering him over to one of the chairs that was secured to the ship infront of her desk and sat him in it releasing him. Her grip on him had been firm but not painful in the least as she assisted him to that point saying as she did so.

“I dunna ken why ye would come here o yer own violation when tis clear yer no sailor nor prepaired fer what ye may er may no find.. an as ta yer reasons ohhh nay lad.. it is na only yer buisness as yer on Me ship...”

by this point shed rounded her desk and stood infront of her chair facing him she placed both hands on the desk looking directly into his eyes..” it be MY buisness as well an yer no goin any place till ye explain..”

a knock sounded on the door “ capin be all well are ye aright ?” she looked at the male seated infront of her his appearance was similar to that of a Drow male in coloring and features however that was where the similarty and compairison ended he was dressed in what appeard to be all black clothing and armor suited to a high ranking lord or better.

With two types of deer like antlers atop his head the smaller more forward aming antlers were tan in coloration where as the higher ones pointed more twords the sky and curved back some were a darker more brownish hew both sets inner twining in places but not quite.

His eyes a silver coloration that remeinded her of her friends but not quite where as Adewens were wolfish his appeared Larger and more serpent like in there puples and shape.

Wyn raised up from leaning on the desk crossing her arms infront of her as she looked at him and answered her man “ Aye all be well ive the matter in hand continue on ta DruidOak we needs resupply afore settin out again..”

There was a long pregnant pause and then the reply “ aye aye capin” the first mate Lachlen turned back to the crew and begain giving orders leaving the captin to deal with the intruder they knew was aboard by scent as well as the breif glimps they had had of him before.

“I be Wynwillow DruidOak lad, an i dunna ken where ye think ye are, but ye be on Easur now an we be almost ta me home. i suggest ye be forth comin an honest lest ye make some enemys ye’d mun rather no”

An anger burned deep inside of him, never had anyone ever spoken to him in such a rude and direct manner, he was both shocked nad furious, his hand shot out almost instinctively as he intended to burn her ship to the waterline, murmering the correct words in his fey tongue.

as a sudden hot wind blew from his hands, and yet which grew was nothing like he originally intended, for it was not fire which climbed the walls of her cabin but instead vines with flowers of every color budding on them, the beings eyes turned curiously from her to his hand as he began to shake it like a broken tool.

The look of anger quickly going to that of perplexion. "I am Arnwyn, Crown Prince of the Fey realms. He attempted to summon a flame in his hand no longer caring about what sort of predicament he was in, a cry of horror escaped his lips as a rose grew in his hand.

To an outsider it would definagtely look as if he was attempting to give Wynwillow a flower, but to him he just sat there in amazement, as the danger of the situation slowly came into his mind, he could no longer defend himself. he decided to be honest, at least to a point, "and i am here because i simply do not wish to be home at the moment, I mean no ill will towards anyone here."

Wynwillow recongized the glint of anger in his eyes and reached for her sword as his hand shot out expecting an attack but she didnt draw it smiling in wary amusement at his confused and horifyed look as apparently what he had intended to happen back fired and flowers begain growing on vines up her cabin walls and while anoying and a pain to remove was not a threat.

she removed her hand from her sword as he spoke and watched him further as he stated who he was, and tryed again only to have a rose appear in his hand she tryed hard not to laugh outright tho it was against her nature to hold back any at all.

she didnt want to anger him further however she couldnt resist..reaching across the desk and taking the rose he appeared to be offering and state " thank ye ill take this as a peace offern o sorts, tho the flowers growen up me walls be a bit much.. they do smell sweet.."

she listened as he spoke further and nodded she could tell from his body language and confusion as well as tone he was telling the truth.

"Vera well lad ill accept what ye ha told me ths far.. an try ta treat ye a wee bit better as ye appear ta be a visitn member o a royal family, given yer manner o dress i ken beleive such.. I be head o DruidOak keep an the people there.. there be no king or monarch o this land we be governed differently. Fer now till ye prove ta be an enemy ill consider ye a frien.. i trust yell no prove me wrong, hower i mun ask.. from where do ye hail ? i ha ner seen one such as ye afor."

He raised an eyebrow, "from the Fey Realms, lands of Leprechuans and fairy folk, are you saying you do not know what i am?" How could she not? He knew what she was and where he was, even if only from books he read while growing up.

"i would think my kind memeroable at least. From what i've read about your peoples our realms had frequent contact in the past. though to be honest i can not remember any time as seeing one of your peoples in our lands." He scratched his head "you are a Damarian right? or did my portal spell backfire like the flowers now growing in your cabin?"

"Nay lad im sorra i dunna ken tho i ha heard stories from visitin the earthly realm o such beins as leprechauns an fairy folk, many o our elders were lost as were many o our books an scrolls durrin an invasion tha happend long ago.. sa i mean no offence but en in me travels ta many other realms i ha ner run across one such as ye afor.. an"

she grinned " aye lad i am a Damarian yer portal didna go awary.." another knock sounded " Come " Wyn replyed and the door opened Lachlen entering " well be dockin shortly capin, be he comin ashore a frien er foe ? " Wynwillow looked from Arnwyn to Lachelen sr.

“he be frien an is ta be treated wi respect due one o the heads o house” Lacheln sr looked at her with a shocked expression and then schooled his features to reveil nothing of his thoughts as he bowed with respect to Wyn and then did the same to Arnwyn, before rising and asking

“be there anythin else ye wish capin? “ Wyn nodded “ Aye sen word ahead ta ha a room prepaired fer our guest an an extra place set a table as well “ Lacheln nodded and left closing the door behind him. Wyn reached for her bottle of previously set aside rum and opened the bottle she poored some in a cup handing it to Arnwyn, and then in another cup for herself.

putting the cork back in the bottle she set it down and lifting her own glass sitting on the edge of her desk she raised her glass to him in a sort of salute saying “ ta becomin friens aye ? drink up lad “ and with that downed the contents of her cup.

Arnwyn eyed the glass with curiosity glimmering in his eye, he had never had any such drink as what as put in front of him. he nodded and lifted the glass to his lips the sweet and burning sensation which left his throat in a quick exhalation was also a new feeling for him.

as he stood the ship seemed to be rocking less, to him it seemed stable as a rock, but to any onlooker he would look as though his body was swaying in tune with the ship. his vision blurred as he stood up, a smile crossing his lips as he stood.

Wyn watching him chuckled and patted him hartly on the back rising with him as he stood “ come time ta head out on deck nothin like the smell o the sea wi the wind an sun on yer face, an home in sight.

“Leading the way out of the cabin she opend the door and walked out on deck watching the preperations for docking Lachlen having things well in hand Saluted her her nodded for him to continue they had arrived.

He followed her on deck to look at the sight of a castle town on a singluar island getting closer and closer, at least he would have seen it were his vision not so blurred, and in a spectuacular fasion he fell head first into the sea.

Toppling over the railing, though at the moment it had not registered that he had fallen off the ship, nor did he realise that he was wet. to him he had tripped over the gangplank which must have been between him and this particularly long dock.

as he stood and began to walking across the surface of the water towards the castle town he could not help but wonder why that particular damarian had a gaelic accent when none of the books ever mentioned such a notable characteristic.

Wyn rushed over to the side diving after Arnwyn but didnt quite reach him before he struck the water she pulled up short and glided up and back around on the air currents.

waiting to see if he would surfice or if she would needs rescue him after all and chuckled shaking her head in amusement as she watched him rise and walk across the water she flew after him and landed next to him once he reached the shore walking next to him up to the keep ..

Chapter 6

Greystone had been home now for sevral years and had come to know thos of his kinsmen that remained, what little of them remained, only 1000 or so give or take a few most of them teens and younglings who had not been old enough to join the battles of thos perhaps 30 not counting Adewen and himself were adults of the Dragonborns themselves that was. The other family branches were in similar strates.

He respected his great neice Adewen who had been head of house until he had challanged her for position. She had filled him in on all that had happened in the past about what her mother had accomplished, and all that had been done in restoring Easur sense.

As little Idri grew she needed her self apointed guardian Wolfen less, and less freeing him to persue his own goals with in his own dragon kind, or with in his adopted family the Stormbringers.

Greystone wasnt sure of him and didnt like him. Why would a Dragon attatch itself to an infant not of its race, nor connected in any other way. However the decision had been made by Adewen before his arrival.

He wondered from time to time if it was not the infant but Ade Wolfen wanted. If so why not make a move. Enough time has passed sense Idri's father had abandoned them. Further more why had Ade chosen the dragon over one of there own?..

However he had caused no harm thus far and had been a good friend to Adewen. all of these thoughts moved through his mind as he flew twords the caverns in responce to the S.O.S signal.. his suspicions were once again surfacing what was going on.

Once he arrived in the training caverns he saw Rhannon had already beaten him there. However unlike Rhannon the only one he did not know was the one who held Idri and Adewen in his arms.

His purple and blue gem like eyes glittered dangerously " RHANNON ! what goes here ? " he took in his great neice, and her daughter in Storms arms idri crying. Rhannon walking tword him swiftly as he landed ready to do battle, but not sure just who or where to start.

Rhannon looked from the one called Storm holding Ade, and Idri to Greystone as he arrived and bellowed her name " Hold Grey we know not yet the full of the situation, but as far as i can tell all here are friendly i was just getting around to asking why Ade sent the s.o.s"

Storm NovaPaw looks at everyone saying what he knew which was not much "she sent it for a reason and was about to tell us when she passed out from helping the Dragon Wolfen, she expanded too much energy in healing him. i'm taking them both to a safer location"

Rhannon nods " we will guard you then as you go." Greystone agreed his eyes softened as he looked at idri. " greetings squirt then hardened as he looked at Ade " is she injured beyond the exaustion?"

Greystone stood 6ft 5inches with a red and white furry body well mucled looking very much like that of a barbarian in body type a well formed tank upon his sholders were tatoos which had been burned into his upper arms black in coloration.

his hair was long falling to his sholders untamed and wild main like black in coloration with red tips at the ends.. his wings were similar to Adewens mothers who had passed in the Bat like red and black coloration. His horns black at the base tapering to red at the tips.. his tail thin and red with a thicker triangular flat point at the end.

He wore what appeared to be a brown furry loin cloth covering his lower extreimitys the animal it was made from was anyones guess, but clean. His wepons two curved swords that to someone of a smaller size would be massive to Greystone were of avrage size.

A wooden shield with metal criss crossing the frame to give it support and add damage if used in combat, rather than defense. He was quite an intimidating figure just to look upon.

Storm shook his head "no just needs rest" Storm looked similar to a Damarian in that he had a fox like appearance and walked upright as they did but that was where the similartys ended.

He had no Wings nor tail they did his horns were more like that of a goats his fur was black and orenge like a dobermens his eyes green and his hair tho short was thick and bright orenge with black streeks, and ears were long almost rabbit like.

Rhannon and Greystone would help to guard Storm as he carried Adewen and Idri from the training caverns they were in.

Rhannon waited until she heard wether Ade was injured, or not then nodded and turned to wolfen" Wolfen what is the danger i smell 4 dragons not just three im guessing the one we cant see yet is the threat"

Storm looked at them both knowing better than to ask how two Damarians thought they could take on 4 dragons even with the help of Wolfen whom Adewen had healed. " keep it busy here my armor is to thick for it to get threw, and i already called for emergancy transport with fighter escorts " once i have Adewen, and idri safe i will return to help."

Grey nods in agreement little idri had stoped crying hearing everyone say mama was ok, and grinned at being called squirt she snuggled up against mama and storm keeping ducked down.

....

Wolfen did not bother with explinations the only two he cared about in the room he knew were in safe hands. He stepped outside he gave a roar a call to arms in and two other black dragons who had brought him to Adewen joined him. The full sun light glazed across the rough surface of their scales, they stared out towards the large like beast of a Red Dragon.

Wolfen Exaimned the dragon and notices the large long claw mark from the side of the dragon that Wolfen did himself before he fell.

The 3 dragons would begin once again another run as they all stretched their wings and took flight into the air with the two dragons following behind Wolfen on either side as they approach the Red Dragon directly.

Heading on a direct course would the Red Dragon, Wolfen would release an roar that would still be abe to be heard from the cave as it wasn't any normal roar, it was like a call but after his roar he spoke in human tongue as he and others charged.

"My brothers! Now is the time for us to show what we are made of!." As he spoke and once again roared, the sudden amount of numbers more roars coming from the oppsite direction of the Red Dragon was more black Dragons.

From Wolfen Home, but Wolfen had this all planned, he was suppose to get himself injured and carried back to Adewen to heal so that the red dragon would follow, so that more of his own kind would come up behind and strike along with the 3 dragons going head on.

Rhannon's head came up eyes glittering as she drew her swords fire coming from her hands up the blades and turning green " Wolfen is a long time firend and ally, but something isnt right there are." Rhannon sniffs the air

"i cant count the number of dragons heading this way .. Storm stay inside the cave im going out to observe from above Grey can you seal up the cavern entranc with your earth abilitys until i can give an all clear ?"

Storm was trying to be reasuring as he said "dont worry about use 4 mins is all i need then air convo is on route with heavy rail guns to help defend the cave entrance"

"Go Rhannon others will be arriving soon having gotten the signal as well so i will watch over those here. " Hearing Storm Greystone shook his head and motioned for Rhannon to go.

Easly keeping track of Storms movements threw the vibrations of the earth and watching over them as they made there way he took them furhter back in the training caverns sealing up the tunnel behind them as Rhannon did what she said she would.

Rhannon flew out of the cavern after watching closely to see that Grey followed Storm and flew up gently flapping her wings to reamin in the air near Wolfens head the sight she saw both impressed, and frightened her. "to quote wyn.. are you bloody well daft ?"

....

Storm got little Idri, and Adewen safely tucked away Greystone nodded to Strom in aproval liking him already, " You should call your people back this is a battle between the dragons we cannot interfear not truly we have given them sanctuary here if your people join the attack it will only draw all of us into there battle and create further havock on Easur." Grey said.

Storm looked at him debating what Grey said but recgonizing the truth of what he was saying he said. " I wont call them back they are needed in another mannor but i will tell them not to engage in the battle only to come here"

Grey looked at him wondering what he ment by they were needed.

....

Wolfen, two dragons behind him and the others that were speeding behind the Red dragon for a suprize assualt, the red dragon would lean its large head down and opens his large jaw as it released it wave of hot flame escaping from its mouth directly at wolfen and the other dragons.

Wolfen and the still bloody stained dragon banked right whilst the other banked left spilting eachother up, but they then came back to going into direct direction towards the Red.

whilst the others from behind would then reach the red and fly under it, in total there were 15 Black dragons including wolfen himself.

Thirteen smaller black dragons attached themselves to the bottom of the dragon's stomach and began to rip the scale layers off from the red stomach eatting their way through. The red would begin to shake its large like floply stomach side to side to wiggle the black's off, but as the red was distracted.

Wolfen flew higher than the other two dragons to then raise his fornt large feet at the red's face. Wolfen attached himself and held tighter making his claws sink deep into the scales.

with his sharp fangs on the side and inside of his mouth, he would began to rip apart the red's right eye ball completely making a like wave of blood pour from its eye socket.

Rhannon watched warily hanging back both knowing from watching this they wernt needed in the combat tho it was hard not to go to the Reds aid even against thos who were there allys, and friends.

Damarians fought fairly when possable there was nothing fair in this battle no battle was plesent to watch, but this wasnt even that this was ... a slaughter.

....

Storm's radio crackles "sir cant get through too many Dragons sir no place safe to land circling arou... Watch out ! " a long moment of silence then it crackles to life once more.. " sorry sir but having to retreat for the time being"

Greystone looked at Storm." Call off your people they arnt prepaired for the likes of us let alone a battle among dragons"

"the main wing coming arnt armed for a fight only escort to gaurd transports which is what i called for they will fly them in the cave and land so that we can get ade and idr to the destroyer in orbit with a medical bay" Storm replyed " however from the sounds of it they had no choice but to retreat."

Storm had Layed Adewen down in as comfortable a place he could find and little Idrialla was sitting next to her mom watching both himself and Greystone intently. she did not look like her grandmother save for her eyes but there was an intellegence there even for her young age and strenght of will that reminded him of her.

"im not sure what a medical bay is but your not putting my neice in one " Greystone stated " we will heal our own.. you said she was not injured she needs rest and energy"

Storm frowned at Greystone arguing with him "and as far as i know shes not but her mind may be from connecting her soul to Wolfens, and i want to run a few tests is all. i've been her guard this long just trust me."

Greystone took the offensive his temper flairing "What kind of tests were not what the humans term gunie pigs"

Storm rolled his eyes throwing up his hands on a sigh " not that kind of test scans mostly to make sure her mind isnt hurt we have a lot of tech that can even heal torn of limbs and such"

Greystone looked at him as if hes insaine shaking his heads no.." i can check that myself with out the need of this medical bay.."

Storm crossed his arms facing Greystone he knew very well what the Damarians could and could not do but he also knew what his tech could do compaired to ... well he suposed Greystone had a point the Damarians had no real need of such devices.

Which was why the wepons they carried and such were still bows and arrows, daggers and so forth they hadnt needed to advance that direction, but he so wanted to see what his scans could find. " you know ether way being her head guard she is my responsiblity"

....

Wolfen would be still chewing at the red eye socket still with the rest of the black dragons chewing at its stomach, but the other two dragons that followed Wolfen would drift down under its fornt.

They released their toxic acid clouds at each of the red's legs slowly as if erasing them but was eatting away rapidly through the scales, muscles and vains as well as bones, it was like the humans called, knife slicing through butter.

Wolfen would then turn to the red's horn and applyed all of his massive weight on the horn and made it snap completely from the red's head making even more blood drip from the head still.

The dragons under the red would detache, and fly out from under it, as they did the red began to fall only one black dragon was caught under the massive weight and curshed instantly dying, but before its head was completely crushed, it let out a loud but very short cry for help as well as pain.

All the black Dragons stop and hovered as well as Wolfen, they looked down as the red crushed him, but the rage and anger of losing a brother to the dragons including Wolfen made them more angered, and more dangerous.

Wolfen as the others flew back and begain was clawing at the red's centre forehead would fly directly on the red's head causing it to to snap back from the impact of Black Dragons clawing and eatting away the head.

Wolfen would emerge having come to through a large bloody hole in the centre of the red's head, and so the black's dragon gathered around with their heads just sticking inside.

They all suddenly released a large and destructive wave of acid into the Red's head instantly melting and erasing it from the inside as it ate away the brain, jaw and skull completely. leaving nothing now but the stump of the neck looking as if like a large massive blade cut off the red's head.

The Black Dragons including Wolfen would be hovering above the headless red before it then leaned to its right and continued as he then slammed its massive large body on to a small forest. The black Dragons and Wolfen hovered over the corpase of the red and growled before then turning and flew back towards the etrance of the caves, 14 returned but one didn't.

....

Greystone was still arguing with Storm " she is of our clan and unless we know her wishes and feelings of the uses of such a device upon her person we can not allow it"

Rhannon shook her head and didnt look at Wolfen or the black dragons she couldnt she waited until they were gone into the training caverns then approched the corpse of the Red.. she begain drawing upon her ability her hands begining to glow red, flames coming to her hands.

Rhannon spread those flames over the dragons body, other Damarians from other branches who had stayed back due to the battle the dragons had been having joined her those with flames helped increese the heat what didnt burn was taken into the ground by those with earth skills and thos with wind helped scatter the ashes to the air.

Storm and Grey turned to face the incoming dragons both prepaired for battle if necessary waiting to see what was to happen now.

Rhannon went herself to the Isles they had given the dragons as safe haven to speak with them of all she had witnessed herself. The Dragons had been allowed to come here to escape being hunted by humans. The Damarians did not interfear in there affairs but when they battled and it spilled onto the rest of Easur, or Thos such as Wolfen tho he was an ally used others to attempt to draw them into choosing sides on such battles.. this could not be allowed.

The dragons would need to come up with there own government among there people of all colorations else they would not have to worrie about the Damarians, Humans or any other races but would kill themselves off in the effort to establish a dominancy among them.

The question was how did they work this so all could live in peace.. and was it too late for reason.

....

The following morning after Adewen woke she felt the call of one of there friends and allys Devon Stormbringer and wearly got up from her bed. After dressing she used one of the crystals to go to him.

As soon as Adewen entered Devons domain Devon begain talking Adewen had not even moved from the spot she had arrived in as of yet " I apologize for not sticking around yesterday" "good mornign m'lord StromBringer " Adewen said bowing politely her voice was soft and calm as ever tho she sounded and looked as tired as she still felt her body trembled slightly from exaustion.

Devon seeing her expression eased up a bit, and gave her time to rise from the bow as he asked " hows little Idri?" Attempting to give her time to recover and explain on her own if she wished rather than bombarding her right away with questions, as to how she had gotten in such a state.

"its quite alright i am glad you came even for a short time i dont remember much after i begain healing Wolfen. " She smiles looking very tired and a bit weaker tho no less powerful " may i sit ? and do you require human form at this time ?"

"you can do what you like hun, doesnt bother me and please, sit I've been creating some things outside for the kids to play in now the snows stopped falling "he laughed a bit, changing the subject to something lighter for a bit.

"Thank you not sure i have the energy yet to take on human form tho i would try if you wished" She moves slowly and sits down listining as Devon speak and smiles in return " good tho i know i treat idri as an adult often, and it is necessary for her to learn so much.. she still needs to be a child as well and i think can do that here"

Devon nodded in agreement with her words tho an expression of some concern touched his eyes watching his friend " yer fine hun I'm curious, is Idri liking Neko?"

"There are other younglings on Easur but difficult for her to play with them which is why i think she likes your Nekos so much. Hes more like her and can have someone to play with her seeing ghosts and speaking with them scares the others at times.."

Devon agreed with Adewens assesment idri was as remarkable a youngling as the Damarians called them as the others. It was hard for her to keep up and play with thos who had wings when she did not.

There were few others that didnt have wings ether but theres were taken from them not born with out them. " I think he likes her too he wont admit it, but i think it so."

"perhaps it is good they are friends she's too adult and she mentioned your wanting Neko to grow up a bit, he can teach her to be more of a child, and have fun and she can help him grow a bit"

"i've always admired your intellegence Ade you grasp exactly what i was thinking and what I am hoping. in the mean time we can continue her training and his if he wishes to participate he may."

Devon poored himself and Adewen something to drink and carried a glass over to her sitting down across from her. " of course I gave Idri a set of iron wood long knives"

"seems were on the same page, and yes i know she showed them to me tho was sad Neko wouldnt spar with her.." Ade greatfully accepted the drink and sipped it slowly.

"well, ive always told Neko we dont hit women"

Adewen set her drink aside and leaned forward a bit as she said "ahh but you also need to teach him to be wary not all women are trust worthy assasins can be women as well as men you know"

he nodded a serious expression on his features for a moment his eyes gleamed " oh I am well aware"

Adewen changed the subject back to the more serious topic they needed discuss. " have you seen or heard from Wolfen this day ?"

"I havent. I am betting he is enjoying time with his Love"

Adewen looked grave and quite serious as she stated " no im afraid not two dragons brought him to me for healing yesteday it took me six hours to heal him i was afraid they might have reached me too late."

“there was a red dragon hunting them i passed out from energy drain just managing to get an s.o.s signal off before hand, and had not had time to ask Rhannon, or Greystone the out come when i felt your summons and came to meet you..”

Devon sat forward then angry more with himself than anything “ If I knew that, I wouldn’ t of left i would have stuck around to help “ Reaching into his vest pocket he hands her a black bag. “here, this should assist”

“it is alright, you had no idea what Wolfen was up to prior to being brought to me for healing then? “ Adewen asked resting a comforting and friendly hand on his sholder.

Accepting the bag in her other hand looking at it. “ what is this ? ” she raises the bag to her nose sniffs at the contents, trying to sort out what is inside.

Devon shook his head no he had no idea what Wolfen was up to. It was odd for ushually he kept himself, or Adewen informed. However nether of them intruded on his personal life or space with out his concent.

“Specialty medicines there is a yellow powder, mix it with whiskey, and it creats a sealant for wounds”

Adewen smiles then laughs a bit “Wyn would enjoy this then”

Devon smiled at her words and shook his head before continuing his explination “ also, a variety of Earth Herbs for sedatives and other needs”

“i will be sure to take it before bed would not due to fall out of the sky half a sleep” she lowered the bag and attatched the string of it to the quiver contining her arrows.

“I hope it helps”

“i can ask Rhannon to join us Grey is watching over idri at the moment Rhannon could tell us what happened after i passed out”

Devon leaned back agreeing wanting to hear more of what happened as well to hopefully be able to make some more sense of it. "of course please do"

Adewen leans back aganst the sofa there is little sparkle in her silvery eyes in stead they held much weryness and worrie. The worrie more for other reasons aside from present issues. she to manages a soft smile.

As she reached for the crystal in her arrow quiver and pulled it out she tapped it emitting a sound freqincy that sounds more like a melody being played.

Not long after a rift much like the ones Idri uses to get back and forth between Easur and Earth would appear. Rhannon step forth.. the rift closing behind her she would take in her surroundings Adewen and Devon and bow politely to her.

....

"Greetings to you both " Rhannon replys her green eyes meeting theres as she arose from the bow her teal colored hair coming down nearly to mid waist Rhannon's settling round her as she straightened, her horns wings and skin were a combination of white's grey's, and black's.

She wore two swords held in place on each leg brown legging's with a white top wich had a leather strap holding it down just under the breast's, leaving her midrift exposed. Her hand's, arms, and face would have soot marks on them from having been working at her forge.

Adewen would start to rise to greet Rhannon in return Rhannon shot her a look. " you should not be up yet, and dont you dare think to greet me formally until your much stronger stay seated Adewen .. i am assuming you called for a reason ?"

Devon looked anoyed at Rhannon's attidude tword's Adewen. Then tryed not to laugh as he reolized she was just concerned for Adewen's well being and as Adewen had not taken offence nor would he. " just social visit so what the hell's happened?"

"i recgonize your scent from idri, and Adewen, but i'm afraid we havent met tho you know of me i am assuming by the same means. I am Rhannon of the BelleRock family branch of Damarians"

She stated offering him her hand when he demanded to know what happened.. "i am assuming you are refering to yesterdays events ?"

Devon looked frustrated, and sheepish at the same time, but remembered his mannors " I'm Devon StormBringer, and I am " he said as he shakes her hand in a firm but gentle grasp.

Adewen spoke up grinning. " of corse he mean's yestrdays event's Rhannon stop beating around the bush and explain"

Rhannon's green eye's danced and she nodded " Very well from what i gathered when Greystone, and i arrived. Strom was holding a passed out Adewen, and little idri who was crying protecting them."

"Storm filled us in on Adewen having healed Wolfen and.." she grew quite remembering the slaughter after... then continued. " Your Wolfen lead the red dragon into a trap purpously leading the Red to Easur tho his reasoinings behind this are as yet unclear. For all Dragons have been given isles on Easur for protection now known as the Dragon Isles.. ."

She looked speculitive and worried about what may occur as a result. They were going to have to set laws so that the Dragons did not interfear with Easur and the Damarians policys but in turn the Damarians would have to stay out of Dragon affairs unless it spilled over onto the rest of the realm.. but that was not a conversation for this time.

"He summoned the blacks who had taken refuge on Easur from humans, and together the red had no chance not even time to fight back it truly was a slaughter.. Grey stayed with Storm to guard over Adewen, and idri until it was safe, while i observed the situation as it took place along with others tho they did not make themselves known until the battles end."

Devon shook his head listining to all Rhannon had to say as he tryed to figure out himself what it was his adopted clans menber was up to. " I see.... Reds are usually violent, but a bunch of blacks.....they dont usually band together.. most chromies are Solitary"

"i am curious i understand why the brought him to me for healing but why deliberatly lead the red to Easur knowing that it is uposed to be nutral grounds. ? " Adewen asked quietly and speculitivly.

"Why indeed you know him better than i. " Rhannon stated " The dragons were allowed to come here for safety away from Earth, and other relms the council agreed to this and to other beings comeing here. What pray tell do you think Wolfens actions will result in?"

Ade cursed not having thought of that before having been too tired after the other days events but Rhannon was correct the origonal dragons realm was closed to those decended from the dragons who had expanded out. " If we can find Wolfen and ask him what provoked the incident and"

Rhannon interupted angry." You think it matters the reason why? There arugment no matter the cause, or reasoning behind it should not have been brought to Easur.." Devon stood gaining both Rhannon, and Adewens attention. " If you please.." when they stopped talking he sat back down saying.

"As it was you specificly Wolfen sought out pheraps you Adewen would be th one they would answer questions of. i doubt they would answer your Greystone's, or mine.. tho they might little idri however i dont think so..as she is so young."

Both Adewen and Rhannon looked specultive but nether spoke they did not need a war with the dragons she wasnt entirely shure who would win out if such occured, but there was a chance.

As the Damarians had not gotten involved in the battle itself they could still claim nutrality. one way or the other aside from Adewen's healing of Wolfen.. they could work something out. Rhannon however was still not pleased over how the battle with the red had taken place..

Adewen thought back trying to remember to sort out the white noise which was what conversations around her became when she healed as she had to remain focused on what she was doing.." i am not sure but i beleive Wolfen is uniting the blacks two at least the ones who brought him to me.. called him lord i beleive"

Devon nodded thinking about what he knew of Wolfen, tho he still didnt understand why Wolfen had wanted to guard over little Idri, not all of what his adopted brother did was clear. "Doesnt surprise me. Wolfen is a drac after all so its possible he is"

Rhannon reamianed quiet and listened leaning against the wall near where Adewen and Devon sat. Remaining quiet and watchful a council meeting would take place once Adewen was recovered fully to address this latest issue.

"Well, as for wounds, I've given Adewen a bag of special medicines, for use there is a bottle of whiskey in there too, but thats for the powder. Dont let Wyn near it .. " He grinned winking at both Rhannon and Ade attempting to liten the mood a bit "Ive made sure to include instructions as well for the various herbs"

"We will not know his motives until one of us is able to speak with him.." Adewen said a bit sleepily already frowning a bit hating being so drained but she would do it again to help her friend she hadnt known how, where, or why he had received the injuries nor aware of the situation only that a friend had been in need.

There was a silence at Wynwillow's name being mentioned but both nodded and smiled tho it didnt quite reach there eyes. They were worried about her being missing Rhannon spoke up " I'll make sure she takes it i've invited her Greystone and Idri to stay at BelleRock until she recovers"

Adewen looked at her..and grinned " how did Greystone take that?" Rhannon chuckled.."About as well as any male when his pride is offended"

"Well, Idri is always welcome to stay here too I know Neko will love that idea" Devon offered he and Destiny as well as the rest of the Storm Bringer pack always enjoyed having Idri around as well as her mother.

He wondered if Idri spent much time with the Ookami pack as far as he knew Lord, now Elder was still struggling a bit at getting the pack to accept half breeds, tho there were not so many now who fought such there were enough.

Adewen smiles " i just may have idri here while i recover she would be safe and be able to have fun rather than worriing over training, or me."

"Very well as you wish Ade. it will be so... However as soon as i get you home your going back to bed.." Rhannon stated and moved to assist her to her feet.

Once back at BelleRock with Ade Rhannon took her streight away up to one of the guest chambers to rest. Rhannon grinned and went to inform Greystone of Adewens wishes concerning Idri going to Earth and the stormbringers care.. Grey was going to blow his top considering Wolfen was apart of the stormbringers if only by adoption.

BelleRock keep was silent this day, something that didnt happen often, aside from the normal conversations, or perhaps slight ringining noises that came from the courtyard where others practiced.

There were no sounds of a hammer striking an anvil, and most of the inhabitant's were down in the crystal mines gathering not only crystals, but other ores and such of use. The aroma of Aden's cooking filled the air as ushaul but un ushually all 10 youngling's were quietly playing in the play room. Sevral adults taking turns keeping watch over them or patroling the grounds.

Adewen slept above resting from yesterdays events recovering her strength. Rhannon was in the library occasionally checking on the younglings, or Adewen as did Aden.

Rhannon was looking over a map on her table that Adewen had given her left behind by Wynwillow before she disapeared. Pondering the meaning's behind the marks upon it. " What are you up too Wyn.." she said to herself.

....

Vukan woke up this morning traveling to Bellerock to see if there is anything he missed after his departure. He had returned to Easur some time ago hoping to see Wyn but had stopped at Firelight village to pay his respects to his head of house, and had stopped by DragonBorn keep to see Adewen only to find she was at Bellerock which was a bit confusing.

Upon landing at the front door, Vukan suddenly feels out of place and unsure. He knocks nonetheless and waits for an answer or see if anyone is up.

Rhannon raised a hand to hault Aden from going to the door hearing the knock upon it. " i've got it Aden youve enough things to do at present." seeing his indignant look she grinned. " what ever your cooking smells wonderful by the by. " at his pleased nodd she went to the door opening it for Vukan.

"Greetings welcome to my home Vukan of the Firelight's tho we have not met formally i have heard of you from Honnora, Adewen, and Wyn before now.. i am Rhannon BelleRock please enter freely"

He bows deeply as he has heard of Rhannon, knowing she is head of BelleRock Keep. " It is a pleasure to meet you as well Rhannon. I, also, have heard of you. Forgive my intrusion this early I was wondering if Adewen was here."

"If she is unavailable I can find her another time. " he rises from the bow. " I appreciated the offer however I am reluntant to enter as the early hour may have not been appropriate for me to show. I apologize."

Rhannon laughed but then grew serious once more as she spoke tho there was still a slight tone of humor to her voice she saw his nervousness, but ignored it.

"she is hear but resting please come inside i will get you something to drink, and see if she is awake she expanded much energy day before and is quite drained, but should be able to receive you."

Vukan wonders having a sudden feeling of having come to a place he should not have thinks perhaps he should go. "Rhannon again I thank you however I am sure she can and should get the rest she needs. I apologize for bothering your household this early, my actions sometimes are without the best judgement. Perhaps I shall take my leave for now ...."

Rhannon shook her head waving a hand dismissivly at this statement. "There is no need for you to do so however if you feel you must i will not detain you. You are welcome here as you are at WhiteOak, DruidOak and all other places on Easur."

She wanted him to know he was welcome " i can assure you it is no trouble my house hold is up often early have no fear you have interupted anything we have already had breakfast but im sure there is some left if you are hungry and would like to eat."

"Perhaps if there is anything you know about Wyn you could part with I would appreciate it. I truly do not feel the need to bother Adewen if she needs her rest." he said reluctently agreeing in part to stay for a short while.

"As you will follow me " Rhannon turned and walked through the dinning hall back into the library expecting him to follow. He did, and looked around him as he went but made no comment. " please sit down and i will answer what i know from Adewen's and myself as well as Honoras discussions todate."

Vukan crosses over to one of the sofas and sits. He was concerned for Wyn hand not contacted him sense they had last spoken it was nearly 6 months sense they had spoken in any mannor which was unushal they had journyed together off and on for 4 years or was it 5 now after she had preformed Devon and Destinys wedding, unless he had had to go assist his sister Laila. "If you would be so kind, I would appreciate that."

Once he was sitting Rhannon smiled, and nodded sitting down herself she rested her elbows on her knees as she spoke her green eyes meeting his colbolt blue one's." Wyn is often carring cargo back and forth as you know. from one realm or another"

"However these trips last anywhere from two weeks to 2 months on the occasions it takes two months she ushually keeps in contact with one, or another of us or sends word threw others friends who have seen her n passing.."

She frowns a bit. knowing she has his attention she continues. "This is where it gets a bit odd.. she stared disapearing for longer lenghts at a time.. but still kept in contact until after the night Adewen heard her cursing about something she was looking for."

"Wynwillow had been pooring over some maps to different realms there were markings on the map Adewen did not see clearly, but that had x's threw them as if she were marking of places she had searched.."

As he listens he hears what is being said concern in his eyes as he had been away from Wyn to go and visit his sister and her new mate Vaul upon earth, aiding them as well as others the Deamos with fighting verious other Earthly demons..

Remaining to aid them in some of there ventures had kept him away longer than he had ment to be so he had no idea where one of the people he cared greatly for may or may not be now, and as far as he knew Icon who had been her first mate was on earth but had been given his own ship to captin. So would not be with Wyn now.. would he possably know where she had gone tho?

"its been nearly a year now with no contact were all very worried but Adewen is tied to the tavern on earth as well as Dragonborn keep.. here on Easur.. i am here as Honnora is at White Oak and so forth there are few adults to spair until the younglings have grown. We are searching when able but limited as we do not know the realms as Wynwillow dose."

Rhannon stood and moved to one of the windows looking out onto a circular plat form where one of the ships she had built was docked.

“The more time passes the more worried we have become i keep expecting her to show any moment with that cocky grin and tell us some tale, or another of her adventure and have us all laughing .. but i fear that isnt the case”

she paused taking a breath she walked over to stand infront of the fireplace before turning back to face him restless..

“You’ve traveld many realms have you not Vukan ? would it be possable for you to search for Wyn where we cannot ? we could send others, but most are not as skilled yet in battle as you who have been out in the verious realms for many years”

Vvukan listens to what is said and contemplates he is hesitent, but also worried for Wynwillow it had taken him centruies to find his sister again how would he find Wynwillow. “ I may. I will have to check things out.”

Rhannon nodded “ Thank you Vukan we would be most greatful Wyn tho she may be stubborn and fearce also tends to have a way of lighting up a room and making everyone around her grin.. when she isnt in a temper..she is missed”

Rhannon studies Vukan lookng him over her green eyes assessing she looks at him curiously” apologies if i am being rude but i noticed you bear no wepons do you rely souly on your elements and hand to hand ?”

“Yes she does do that. “ he smiles his thoughts obviously far away for a bit remembering something in the past. “ No I do not rely solely on elements and hand to hand “ I do have a couple swords however. I find here within the keeps I have no need to carry them all the time.”

He shakes his head “ Most times I can get what I need done without them. so perhaps you are correct i do rely on them instead “ He laughs at his own words.

Rhannon smiles “ very true may i see your swords if you do not mind i’d like to reinforce them with Damarian steel and strenghten them” “you may however I do not have them with me at the moment, also one is a lightning blade not sure if you will be able to reinforce it but you can have a go at it, i thank you for the offer.”

Rhannons green eyes dancing at the challange replyed. “ ohh indeed i can i may even add a bit of something to your other sword. Her mind was already turning thinking about what she would need what components and so forth and cursed that he didnt have them here for her to examine so she had a more firm fix on what she could do with them..

Vukan bows respectfully as he says “ Thank you”

Rhannon was drawn out of her musings by his action and words “ your most welcome Vukan please bring them to me when you have time i have a feeling when you find Wynwillow you may need them.”

“I am but one when there are more looking for her. I am sure one of the others will find her before I am even close “ He looked worried but could only prey she be found be someone wether it be him or not soon.

“I shall bring them by when I can. “ noticing the suns position has risen from when he stopped by. “ I thank you Rhannon for the information and offer to help with weapons. Please let Adewen know I give my best. I am afraid it is time for me to get going. I look forward to another meeting.”

Rhannon raised a hand to stop him “ one moment before you go “ she motiones for him to follow her once more turning twords another door way that lead out of the library. “ please follow me there is something else i would give you”

before turning to leave he says “I will see what I can find out regarding Wyn and will keep in touch. “ he stops seeing her raised hand and puzzled he looks at her and follows her from the room.

Rhannon nods in thanks at his paitence and leads the way to her work room in the former dungon. she walks over to a chest and opens it to take out one of the may crystals inside it is large enough that it filled the palm of her hand.

“this is one of the communication crystals “she stated and proceeded to show him how it works by explaining.

“different tones when it is struck will iminate a sound wave that will create an s.o.s signal, or in striking it in verious other ways signal specific house holds to a need to communicate as well as one other frequincy when struck that would open a small rift for travel to one realm or another a protective barrier will form around you as you go through the rift.”

“the crystal works indefinatly for s.o.s sigals or alerting one house hold or another of your need to speak with one of them however. these smaller crystals unlike the ones that power our ships have only 2 to 4 trips in them back and forth from one realm to another.”

Vukan smiles as he takes the crystal offered. Doing his best to remember what he had been told and shown. “ It reminds me of the ones my father left with me when he told me to protect Laila, I still have a couple left and only knew how to get them to transport me from one realm to another. I thank you for teaching me how to communicate. I will make sure I use them and hopefully never for s.o.s.”

touched by this he strides to her and hugs her whispering a thanks than steps back. “thank you for the crystals Rhannon. I shall be in touch. I shall take my leave and see myself out. “ He puts the crystal into his pocket turns and walks out of dungeon to the outside where he takes flight and leaves Bellerock.

Rhannon stiffened in his arms at his hug not used to having others outside her family branch or perhaps Honnora or Wynwillow hug her. She waited until Vukan left then walked back twords the other side of the keep checking on the younglings who were playing leaning up agaist the wall watching them a while.

Chapter 8

Checking in on Adewen seeing that she was resting comfortably and soundly Rhannon left her be and made her way twords the front of the keep to check on Aden to see if he needed help in the kitchen with prepairing the afternoon meal. The others hadnt returned yet still working in the mines.

The earth began to rumble around the BelleRock Keep, Thunder and lightning of the purest blue cracking like a whip in the distance. Soon a massive bolt of Amethyst colored lighting strikes the main courtyard, splintering the stone as an amethyst flame erupts to life, surrounding a single figure in purple see through robes.

His every muscle rippling fluidly as he stretches and looks around. He was told this is where the Keep was and where he would find the Lady Adewen and Lady Rhannon. His skin was tannish, his hair long and silver and his eyes.

His eyes were of the deepest purple, endless in their vast experience and mysticism. ON his back he wore a battle axe made from a strange material. he looked around with an intense gaze, an aura of power and allure surrounding him, his mere presence weighing down on the keep.

Rhannon had only just started across the court yard to the kitchens when the ground shook her bright grass green colored eyes flashed dangerously as an unkown scent and presense filled the air.

Aden appeard in the entry way oposite her as the flash of lighting struck the courtyard the lighting crackling all around eccoing in the small area. The younglings in the far chamber cryed out and rushed out to see what was happining Rhannon held up a hand and called.

"Stay back ! " seeing them as she turned to sheild her eyes from the flash created by the lighting they obayed and remaind back.

Aden had been knocked from his feet and was just standing as the male was reveilded the lighting stopping. Rhannon drew her swords as Aden drew a sworl of air to one of his hands prepaired to defend if needed.

Adewen feeling the energy from the being arriving awakened in the upper chamber where she had been resting and forced herself to get to her feet.. to make her way out onto the walk way above the courtyard.

Her long white hair flowing around her, silvery eyes taking in what was happining below as Rhannon approched the glowing male.." Who are you stranger what brings you to BelleRock on Easur ?"

He looks around at the ones who seemed to have appeared from the depths of the Keep. With a single motion, a blur to the eyes of those around him, he draws his battle axe and slams it onto the ground head first, holding onto the handle of it as his purple eyes flashed momentarily.

He offered a soft smile despite his powerful presence and let go of the hilt so that it could fall onto the ground with a clink to show he meant no harm. " Greetings. I am Lord Strykerious, Successor of the Lord Ryu." With that he bows to them.

Rhannon as he drew the battle axe had taken a defensive stance automaticly flames shot up from the palms of her hands up the blades of her swords. Aden awaited a signal from her before acting.

Adewen had awakened and was on the battlements above overlooking the court yard expanded her wings and glided down to land not far from Rhannon as the axe struck the ground.

All eyes watched him closely relaxing, and looking at him curiously with puzzled expressions tinking it a trick of some sort, as he released the handle and let it fall to the ground showing them he ment no harm.

"stand down Rhannon Aden.. he isnt hear to harm anyone.. " Rhannon and Aden looked at Adewen then at each other, and the male. Rhannon nodded to Aden trusting in Adewen's jugement.

The flames upon her wepons died down, and she resheathed her blades Aden dispersing, and releaeing the air element he had gathered back into the natural flow..Rhannon spoke up..

"What goes here Ade ? " Adewen looked at her.." The one he suceeds was my adopted father Ryu.. the only one of the void guardians that did not abandon us.."

Rhannons eyes flashed dangerously, and angerly the void guardians had abandoned them when Easur had been invaded " your telling me hes a void guardian ?"

He tilts his head " I am Not just any Void Guardian... I am a full on Void Lord now.... We did not abandon you, we had helped to reclaim the land that Idrialla was fighting to reclaim, allowing her to gain it back. MY predescessor cared very much for your race... for Adewen and Idrialla the most though..."

Rhannon fairly shook it took all she had in her not to draw her swords again.. Allow ...allowing her to gain it back.. she managed a small grin.. tho her hands were fisted as she said. " its for respect for the ONE void guardian who didnt abandon us i dont attmept to run you threw now..."

Aden moved from where he was to Rhannon's side he was an elder his hair, and beard grey and silver tho he still held no less power in his form. He remembered the Void guardians as friends and allies and the betrayel.

He knew how powerful a full fledged void lord if he was as he said could be, there were not enough of them to take him on at present if he chose to attack. Aden nodded respectfully to Ryu's replacement.. as he rested a callming hand on Rhannons sholder.

Strykerious chuckled a bit amused by the Green eyed ones words " If you wish to attempt to run me through, if it would make you feel better about it.... I am sure Adewen can sanction it"

Adewen shook her head stepeing between Ryu's successor, and Rhannon as Rhannon stepped forward her hands going to her wepons. Rhannon stopping only as Adewen was in her way.

"i am not head of house here at Bellerock to sanction such. It is in fact Rhannon who is head of house hold here however. i will interveen, and stop this before it gets out of hand to keep the two of you from battle."

"it is an honor to meet my stepfathers sucessor may you do him justice. As you are here dose this mean he has passed ?? " Rhannon not liking Adewen's interfearance, but aware she has the cooler head at the moment, and that this fellow ment no real harm at presnt cursed under her breath stepping back.

He looks down, his eyes darkening in grief as he stares down at the ground. He speaks, his voice full of pain and sorrow." As he and his brother did before,... He faded.... this time i feel it is permanent....."

Tears come to Adewens silvery eyes as she nods sadly " Thank you for brining this news often when one died the other took his place between the two, but i trust in your words when you say they are both lost it must be so my step father never mentioned you before how is it we have not heard of you ?"

He looks over to the Lady Adewen and sighs heavily. " I am a well kept secret... If enemies knew i was to succeed him in his time of Fading, they would know he was getting weak and a war would break out in the Void..."

"As it is, i am thrust into the title before my time, and will not be of much use until i am able to sway more of the void guardians to my, our way of thinking for themselves rather than simply following orders mindlessly with out question."

"i see you have my grattitude for speaking with me on this matter i cannot speak for Rhannon or the others as many feel as Rhannon dose about the void guardians, but you are welcome to Dragonborn keep, and may visit as often as you wish. As well as welcome at my tavern on earth.. " Adewen said. Little did she know that after this visit they would not see him again until much much later after little Idri had grown.

Rhannon's anger twords the void guardians was only partally warnted she knew this and sighed after all this one hadnt done anything to warrent her anger " you are welcome here as well i will try not to judge you by others actions, and know you for yourself .. please forgive my earler hostilitys"

He nods to Rhannon, and cannot help himself as he comments " If its any help, which i doubt it would be... I found your hostility amusing, definitely a brightener on my day." He chuckles light heartedly before looking around and speaking once again.

"Unlike my predecessor, I control the light, am more apart of the light then the darkness, though we both are made up of the extremes of darkness and light. As you knew, he favored the darkness, i favor the light but seek solace in the darkness at times.."

Adewen couldnt help grinning for so like her step father this fellow was full of contridictions that connected, and even so still made a kind of sense. Rhannon simply gave him a look crossing her arms over her chest.

Aden next to her tightinging his hold on her sholder a silent warning to keep her temper in check she grinned also simply saying. "you find me amusing i find you arrogant however so long as you bring no harm to me or mine and reamain a friend to others i will welcome you."

he chuckles a bit and looks over to the ever seeming hot headed one known as Rhannon and smiles at her. " Arrogant you say? hmm It seems i have more in common with my Predecessor then i thought."

"Aye i am Arrogant, but arrogance is just arrogance without the skills to back it up, as for me... I have no need to be full of hot air. However, you can keep your temper if you want, i find it quite hot if i might say so myself." He winks at her then back at Adewen. " I am sorry i was kept a secret but it was to hide his weakness"

Adewen looked at Rhannon as if she had lost her mind but then chuckled at the guardians replys in turn. Rhannon blushed then bowed and turned to leave them all to check on the younglings who were now crowding in the door way behind them.

She spoke with them quietly manovering them back to the play room answering questions they asked as she went suggesting a game to paly and so forth. Aden spoke then.." i shall excuse myself to return to finnishing fixing lunch will you remain lord ? " he asked waiting quietly as Adewen spoke once more " its hard to immagine the one who trained me having any weaknesses"

He looks over to Aden and nods before returning his eyes to Adewen " Aye he was very powerful, but time and heartbreak and heartache wears even the strongest down to a fragile form."

"He was fragile when he began to take me on. Among those he could have chose, i was the one... he claimed... that the Fates had destined to take his place. I do not know why but i guess in time i will find out"

"indeed that is quite true.. i look forward to getting to know you sir " Aden nods and moves off to the kitchens it isnt long before the sound of a hammer striking steel on an anvil begins ringing threw the area.

Adewen smiles at the curious look on the fellows features and begins explaining. " that will be Rhannon shes gotten the younglings settled it seems and has returned to her work room would you care to see it i can show you the way"

He nods and looks around the Keep and sighs a bit before tilting his head and smiling to her. " i look forward to getting to know you as well... I was told to visit, and as i was told..." looks in the direction of Rhannon and then at Adewen. " The beauty of the Damarian's is astounding."

It was Adewens turn to look curiously at him as she asked " Told to visit and who could order such as you aside from another of your kind? " Adewen asked curiously leading the way to Rhannons work room.

He follows her as she leads the way and looks around the sounds of other Damarians returning to the keep from other places begain filling the hall in the background as they moved through out the keep prepairing to clean up for the meal ahead.

"Believe it or not, it was Ryus last wish... He told me to look for Dragonborn or related Damarian keeps... this one was the closest. He told me to give his best wishes to his Daughter...he did not say anything about adopted. I guess you were like his own flesh and blood... It is good to know that on his last breath he smiled at the thought of his old family"

Adewen paused she had loved Ryu very much in so many ways he had been more a father and mentor to her than her own father had, and she would miss him greatly"

He was not blood kin but was more of a father to me while i was growing. Tho i am slowly coming to know my birth father better. Ryu until the invasion was with my mother and gave me two brothers that were lost ... thank you.."

she blinked back tears and smiled as they came round the corner entering the work room Rhannons hammering paused as she looked up at them catching there scents before they entered.

Her green eyes met theres she nodded to them and then turned to heat the wepon she was working on in the fire there were soot smudges and sweat across her brow she picked up a rag to wipe her hands before speaking " is all well ?"

"aye all is well " Adewen replied grinning. " your clammoring brought us to you as you did not return to join us"

"i see i supose its is as i deserve having you invade here as i forgot my mannors.." she motioned twords the bench " your welcome to stay if you can stand the noise. i'll most likely be here threw lunch unless Aden drags me away.." Rhannon stated to which adewen spoke.

"Aden wont have to this time i insist you stop to eat Rhannon at least so long as im here .." Rhannon sighed but nodded in agreement. knowing Adewen wouldnt leave go and she wouldnt get any peace to get the work done other wise. " very well my work will just have to wait"

He chuckles a bit and looks at Rhannon with a smile " I myself am a bit of a blacksmith"

"ohh ? " Rhannon asked real interest other than as a potental enemy sparked in Rhannon's eyes her interest captivated. Adewen raised her hands laughing and left the two of them be, knowing when to give in.

Rhannon launched into discussing smithing and the vaerios metals and the differeances between earth and other realms metals and Easurs so on and so forth Adewen later returning to interupt them letting them know lunch was to be served.

....

storm wevers ship : " sir we followed Wynwillows ship per your instructions shes moving from realm to realm searching for some type of crystal ether she isnt as good as you thought or is too distracted and dosent care shes being followed. still we try to remeain out of her way unless needed she and her crew have gone inside a cave of sorts in this sector of Earth of all realms.

there battling there way inside thos they fight look like damarians sir.. they are weilding elements, and such similar to Wyn and thos of her kind were prepairing troops to give aid...one looks alot like her an older male... Theyve gone inside the caves.."

a loud explosion could be heard over the com it would be some time due to the interfearance in the air from the force of the blast before the captins voice could be heard one again " sir .. the cave wyn and her crew everyone inside it .. its exploded.. once once the fires die down sir well search the debrees, but sir its unlikely there were any survivors.. as soon as its safe to do so we will land sir and search the area..

what happened inside the cavern between there entry and the explosion..

The ocean breeze fluttered through the leaves of the trees causing the branches on which Shames was sitting on to sway gently back and forth. He was a tiny little man, about 3 inches tall with a pair of green leggings and a smart looking brass buttoned green jacket to match.

He looked out over the beach to see the landing party of weird fox demon looking things coming ashore.

he watched with slight interest as the eager looking bunch pulled their boats off the surf and settled themselves on the beach quickly forming battle lines with bows drawn and swords flashing, glinting the rays of the sun in all directions.

"I never saw reason in my life to wear such ridiculous armor and such," he said ideally, "but then i don't get hurt easily."

he waggled his legs back and forth as he continued to watch their hurried movements, curious in part for what they were doing in a realm where they obviously did not belong, and also for why they were here on this particular island.

Wyn looked around her as they came ashore gliding on the air currents along with her crew the breeze siring her shoulder length hair that tapered to Grey and black at the ends the tiny chains that adorned her horns swaying back and forth with her movements.

"o all the damn realms i ha searched hunt in um down.. tis earth i come ta i the end.." she shook her head her expression serious as she wondered briefly how everything seemed to circle back to this realm.

Be that as it may she had to set things aright and they wouldn't be escaping this time round she directed her crew to spread out staying in groups of two or three to search the isle while her new first mate Lachlen Sr. moved to her side.

she advanced drawing her sword from her back words the falls as the others fanned out to the right and left to search Lachlen and two others following her she gathered energy to her hand feeling it grow as she took hold of some of the air currents.

she paused before the falls her ears turning this way and that as she listened scenting the air her pink eyes closing as she gathered what information the winds would bring her.

Shames eyes centered on the blue fox like demon, he watched as she neared the falls her red and gold frock flapping in the wind created by the rushing water, her sword straight out in front of her almost as if she were cutting a course through the air and mist which began to swirl around her as she approached.

Wyn's head tilted to the side a bit the scent of the leaves sand salty air, grass's, animals and the like seemed to wash over her a moment as she sorted threw the information given her. her eyes opened slowly.

a serious expression upon her features along with a half grin as she let out a whistle and the rest of the crew that had fanned out returned falling instep the sand shifting beneath there steps as Wynwillow raised her hand words the falls.

The air shifting and moving parting the falls like someone were pulling drapes apart to gaze out a window behind the falls appeared to be a cave like entrance Lachlen looked over at her. "Capt in it could be a trap.."

Shames leaned forward knowing what sat on the other side of the falls he leaned listening anxiously for the explosions and shouts of a good brawl to start, he always liked that sort of thing.

He listened carefully knowing the most opportune moment would be, which was obvious to him, as they crossed the falls into the cave, the added annoyance of the water hitting them would increase the level of chaos and the noise of the falls themselves would help the chaos ensue.

He suddenly lost his balance because he was leaning to far forward so that he quickly fell forward from the branch plummeted like a pebble from a cliff down to the ground in a very soft almost unheralded "squish."

"Aye lad.. it Vera well may be a tha... hower.. we canna le the crystal be used fer foul means." With out another word or glance at the crew and Lachlen she advanced knowing with out question they would follow.

Lachlen winced when she called him lad he had worked his way up threw the ranks to become second mate under Icon but she hadn't noticed him any more than the rest of the crew one day he thought.

His attention turned back to the situation at hand as they entered the cave behind the falls threw the parted curtain of water there captain had provided.

The cavern which awaited them was much larger inside then it was at the mouth, though its dark recesses were hidden in the shadows. Except for what light filtered through the waterfall, and a faint glow far off in the back of the cavern.

The cavern was pitch black. as the party of Damarians moved into the cavern just beyond the entrance a large silhouette stepped forward to block their the dim glow of the distant crystal whose coloration had already began to change from a blueish green to a very deep red, the colors swirling around the cave seeming to almost be fighting each other for dominance until the red overtook the blues and greens.

The silhouette raised its arms and other lights began to show around the group from the walls, except these lights quickly became apparent.

As that being the burning tips of flaming arrows notched and drawn back on bows ready to be loosed at them. The light from the fires reached the face of the silhouette, his dark violet eyes glared at Wyn, a very easily seen anger crossed his blue furred face.

"i should have expected as much, that a being of such disappointment would dare to show its face at the most inopportune time." he brought his hand down to rest on the hilt of his blade, from where it had been holding his head in hopes of staving off the headache of a daughter whom he had once called his own.

"Why can you not just know your place like your sisters, you've always been such a dire disappointment, but fear not child, though i may have failed to put you back where you came from," he drew his sword and signaled them to fire as his words echoed off the walls of the cavern "I'll surely speed you on to your next destination"

"Ye can try bu as ye noticed I'm no a chil any longer.. an I'm na afraid o ye.. have a me if ye can? " The anger she got the thicker her accent her eyes glittered in the lighting of the caverns her sword still in hand.

she as well as the others hand noticed the changing in the crystals glow and knew they didn't have much time, and they needed more information but unless her father was in the mood to share she knew questioning him would be pointless.

so letting out another whistle to signal her crew to attack as she lifted her hand in front of her spinning it as she took hold of the air currents to swirl them together threw out the cavern creating a vortex that would go before her and her crew.

As they advanced not only blowing out the flaming arrows but sending sending them flying ripping them from the archers hands splintering them against the stone walls of the cave her crew engaged those who managed to keep there feet while Wyn engaged her father.

Her father raised up his sword and sent the many minions which lined the walls of the cavern charging forward their elemental magics sending lightning bolts, fire orbs, and icicle shards flying as they lept towards Wyn's crew.

While he himself stepped back waiting for either those that currently served him to finish off her crew of peasants and corner Wyn, or for them to be cut down awaiting his moment to crush his rebellious daughter and rid himself of this annoyance.

Wyn's crew wielded there own elements as well melting ice shards deflecting fire and lightning orbs words the falls a faint hissing sound heard as they hit the water cascading down.

The sounds of swords and clashing would be drowned out by the roaring of the falls " aww runnin away from me are ye da.. ner thought ta see the day ye'd back away from anyone le alone yer own wee daughter"

Shames wriggles his way free of the bush and thicket he had fallen into. He stopped to pluck thorns the size of his leg, seeing as how he was 3 inches tall, out of his arise before coming to stand up on the top of a bush and poke his head out the top.

jerking and jiving as he watched the brawl happening through the falls, every now and then a bolt of fire would make it out of the falls and plummet down into the stream leaving a sizzling stem cloud to ride down towards the ocean.

Her father quickly turned around upon reaching the crystal and raised the amulet which the void guardians had given him to corrupt the crystal with towards Wynwillow.

a smile touched his lips once he had lured her to within the ring of iron deposits which sat deeper in the cave, as he called forth as much power as he dared. "goodbye little pest" and with that a veritable wall of lightning coursed out of his hand reaching in all directions.

Filling the cavern with blinding light as the electricity which continued to flow from the amulet arced across the cavern wall slowly turning the iron into white glowing molten slag. and with a slight shoving movement the wall shot forward towards Wyn, the electricity arcing off of the stone as it sped towards her.

Wyn fought her way past one of the other Damarians that followed her father Lachlen on her heels..guarding her back. she realized something was wrong as her father lead her closer to the crystal before turning to face her.

He raised some sort of amulet towards her she dropped her sword and raised both hands as her father spoke she created a swirling barrier of air around herself. Lachlen had fallen behind engaged by another.

With one hand she kept a swirling barrier around her, with her other hand thinking quickly she created another funnel to draw water from the falls and redirect it towards the glowing molten slag coming at them Lachlen called out to the crew in warning but too late..

As the funnel drew the water inside, it flowed out the tip in a jet stream of super cooled super pressurized water which opened a gaping hole in the wall of molten slag to neutralize the electricity which had been speeding through it.

as the jet stream flew back towards her father he only had enough time to have a shocked look on his face before he was soaked enough for the electricity which flew out of his hand to arch back and flow back to the crystal castling a chain reaction.

which caused the crystal and explode, and while he flew through the air towards the wall of molten iron he had flung at his daughter his look of shock turned to horror.

His thoughts turned to him being proud of her cleverness, before beings melted down and having his blackened bones go shooting through the wall and out the cave entrance.

Wyn and Lachlen were blown backwards threw the gaping hole that had been opened in the slag as it flowed past them encompassing the rest of her crew and what was left of the other Damarians that had served her father.

a peace of the crystal caught Wynwillow along the forehead cutting her temple as she was blown back into Lachlen. who wrapped his arms round her he felt her go limp afraid she were dead.

The last thing he remembered was the spray of water as they passed threw the fall and then nothing as they hit the ground and sand below being blown past the pool of water at the falls base.

Shames dodged the molten slag droplets as they came showering out of the cavern opening and fell into the water pool below. The force of the bellowing steam causing Shames to be knocked back into the thicket again.

Making him squeak in a not so pleasant sounding way as he was nearly run through by the massive thorns. He soon shook himself free and unstuck himself of all the impolite little buggers which had made him look like an inverted porcupine.

after which he stopped only to pinch out a single flame which burned on the edge of his waxy curled mustache. He walked down to where the blue Damarian female lay limp next to another badly burned one.

He tapped them both with his foot to be sure they were both still alive. While doing so he noticed how badly his coat had been burned, the brass buttons were black and miss sharpened from the heat. “while that may be one thin less to be worry in about ya owe me a damned coat ya blue flea bitten fox”

Wynwillow slowly awakned upon the beach she felt disconnected from herself and was having trouble making her limbs even move it took her some time to open her eyes.

She had no idea how long she had lain there it was night there were stars in the sky the air was cold the sound of waves lapping the shore line as they drifted in and out reached her ears.

The world spun as she managed finally to sit up she nearly passed back out her head felt as if it might explode. Touching her hand to her temple she felt an injury there and alot of blood some of it was dry. Where was she.. what had happened.. for that matter who was she..?

Her vision and mind begain to clear a bit as she looked around her the scent of death burnt flesh and more carried on the breeze.

Seeing the bodies of others around her, she crab walke backwords her breath caught in her throat her chest tight she turned over onto her hands and knees scrambling to her feet as she tryed to flee the sceen.

Running blindly not knowing or recognizing anything she didnt know how far shed gone but collapesed near a river her breathing harsh and rappid not only from the shock but the run. She jumped alert to the sound of tree branches snapping an grabbed for a wepon instinctivly only to find none.

A male with burned skin steppe dout of the tree line calling out to her " Capin" as she watched him approch she could tell from his expression he appeared to know her and was adresssing her as captin.. did he hold the answers she sought ?

Lachlen could see wyn had no idea who she was and didnt remember what had happened nor why. He waged an internal battle to tell her the truth or not. He had no chance of winning her over.

Before she hadnt even noticed him he was as any other crewman to her, now tho he had a chance to start over " Capin Faeril tis me Lachlen yer first mate.. Les ge ye back ta the crew an be on our way the battle be oer."

When she appeared a little hesitent he continued " i cen see yer confusin capin bu once our wounds be tended i ken explain le us ge out o here" She didnt know wether to beleave him or not but knew staying here wasnt an option ether.

Once on board ship she begain to relax some as the crew did indeed refer to her as captin and begain to feel more at home on the deck of the ship at the healm and in her cabin she was just a bit frustrated at the fact that she couldnt remember a damned one of them.

Lachlen was the only damarian left alive aside from Wynwillow after that battle the rest of the crew that had remained on ship were lycons vampires and other types of creatures. it was pure luck that had saved his and wyns life at all.

Now he only need get the rest of the crew to agree to go along with calling her Faeril by telling them as a result of her head injury she beleived this to be her name, and calling her other wise would only confuse her and do more harm than good in time her memorie would return and just to go along with it till then.

Another watched them from the shadows aside from the little green fellow, someone whos scent Lachlen caught and took note of a scent that had been present at the battle in the cave. so one of them escaped.

He could use that to his advantage and send the captin after him to keep her asking too many questions, it was likely this being would want revenge anyway for the loss of his companions as well.

little did Lachlen know now however he had to get them out of there before that ship that had been following them landed to investagate.

Chapter 9

A year later...

"I don't like being followed you know " a male smirks as he knows someone has been following him-

Faeril sence finding out about what had happened to her old crew had been tracking a fellow who had escaped the blast as she and her first mate Lachlen had seen him flee as she had been struck down, and burned.

she had tracked him to an accurced realm in habbited by Titans and Giants vichous beings that ate the fleash of anything smaller than them.

she took them down bit by bit one at a time when necessary and tracking him she wasnt ready to attack him yet simply studying him she smiled but remained silent where she was

The male continued to smirk as he crossed his arms and sighed, if she wasnt going to come out then better shine some light on the subject. A seal of gold and energy of the light suddenly appeared and grew on the ground.

Surrounded a five mile raidus around. All shadows and darkness within this seal would of been expelled and everything hidden would of been revealed including someone hiding in the shadows.

Faeril stood no sence in hiding now she came from around behind the tree with out a sound most of her body hiden completly coverd save for parts of one arm and the area between her chest and neck " why did ye blow up the cavern me n me crew were in...?"

He didn't turn round to face her, his white and black hair blowing in the gentle breeze he laughed a bit. "we didnt blow it up you did.. and they deserved to die for there betrayel of the Void Guardians all of you do..."

"an what betrayel prey tell were that ? " she asked with out a sound her daggers cleared there sheath's she could easly do one of 3 things if she cose block attack or throw. with out a word Faeril moved in.

Her foot steps if any could be heard at all were light and swift she held her daggers one along her wrist the other out as she aimed for his ribs keeping the other up to block.

"Pathetic " Out of the seal in all directions shot pillars of pure, deadly, almost holy light. The pillars creating a maze of light around her and Salome, seperating the two from view

Faeril cursed if only she had manage to scratch him just a bit the poison on the tips of her wepons could have done the rest tho wether posion worked on this fellow or not was another matter.

Given he also had lycon dna by the scent of him...ther was a chance it would..she followed her nose now so to speak shething her daggers and drawing her bow and arrow instead

Coming out of one of the maze wall's shot a whip of light, aiming for the back of her right heel.

Faeril lept up pushing off the wall with one leg spinning and firing down. Pinning the whip to the ground before she landed reaching up she removed her hood but contined.

he clapped, then removed his shirt and jacket now revealing his torso but also the two brace's on his arms. His arms covered in a dark, devilish energy.

Faeril turned her pink colored eyes to him hearing him clap there was alot of hatred and anger in them aimed his direction.

she quickly drew another arrow and fired aiming for the middle of his chest so that even if he moved left right up or down he would be hit.

He Grinned as he caught the arrow with ease, his eyes closed

she quickly followed it up by 5 more moving closer with each shot before rushing forward with blurring speed leaping over to the side running along the right wall bow still in one hand dagger in the other.

He opened his eyes a look of fearce intent in them as well as grudging admiration. as she advanced.

Out of his left hand, at the end of all four fingers and his thumb shot thin whips of light, slashing the arrows in half like they were tooth picks.

As he got rid of the arrows Faeril closed the distance leaping off of the wall landing behind, and to the side of him she ducked low. Bringing her bow down behind and across his knees in a sweeping jesture to knock him from his feet.

While aiming for his throat with her dagger intending to impail him with it. Should she miss as he went down she could always change the angle of her dagger and it s direction.

With a sigh both her weapons went through him like he wasn't even there, his body shimmering a little as her weapons passed through him before he walked a few steps ahead. taunting her with his words " Light is both solid and not"

Faeril growled how the hell did one fight light.. she would have thougth with the absance of it, but she had been watching him and knew he was both she was not ready for him not yet. Best to disengage and try again when better prepaired.

She flipped backwords putting further distance between them her pink colored eyes narrowed on him.. " we arena done.. i will return.." with that she unfruled her wings intending to return another time she needed to plan better and think.

"I disagree " Holding out his right hand three whips of light shoot forward and wrap around her ankle, the light burning her flesh as two other whips wrap around her throat, restricting her breathing and burning her flesh as well.

Faeril brought her bow up in time to block the whips that shot out to wrap around her throat and already was leaning forward to slice threw the one warpped around her ankle, then the rest deftly and swiftly.

"dis agree all ye like.. " cut free she tossed her bow aside as the whips had firm hold on it and drew her sword now armed dagger in one sword in the other.

The male shook his head as he grabbed the two rods on his braces, the two rods sprouting dark spikes before a blade shoots out of the front of them.

Fareil watched him closesly as he drew his blades he was impressive shed give him that, and handsome but he had killed her friends thos who had given there lives in following her.

Had he even sought proof of there suposed crimes or just followed orders like a good boy.. ohhh how she was angry, no one killed her crew, and who were these Void Guardians he had metnioned.

smirking as he jumps up at her, moving at surprising speed. he held his blades tightly, and poised them for a battle.

she brought her blades up to block as he came at her sparks flew a shock reverbrated from the clash shaking the pillers that had formed of the maze he had created

He looks into her eyes, swinging his body in a down ward arch, sending his right foot towards her ribs.

The realm she had tracked this being to had isles chunks of land that floted in the air seprate from the realms planet structure some were large enough to hold castles but little else others were simply smaller moving masses.. few holding trees or were small bowls which held floating lakes that when it rained became moving water falls as they over flowed onto the land below.

They fought in a clearing on the gorounds below surrounded by giant trees and bolders, what sort of other beings lived in this realm she had no notion nor did she care she had only come tracking this being here. The only thing keeping them from distroying the landscape around them was the maze of light he had created that they fought inside of.

Faeril spun as his foot turned in twords her ribs her blade sliding along his as she disengaged her dagger when she spun intending to hit him in the back of the head with its hilt.

Still smirking he ducked his head a little further down so the attack missed, using the momentum to quickly change directon, and send a punch towards her gut he was both impressed and amused with her.

The blow landed she gave a small grunt, and nodded her head in acknowladgement of the hit and brought her knee up into his ribs.

A grunt came from the males lips as he dropped his blades, this was now a battle of the bodies alone. Clenching his fists tightly he sent another to the other side of her ribs.

Dropping her dagger she grabed the back of his head as he hit her in the ribs once again and head butted him hard if her ribs wernt cracked they would defanatly be brused and hurt like hell when the adrennile wore off if she survived this.

A louder grunt of pain escaped his lips as blood trickled down his forehead, still he smirked as he sent his elbow at her, aiming for the left side of her jaw.

She leaned back shoving him away narrowly missing his elbow she kicked out at him aiming for his left hip.

Grabbing and hooking his left arm around her leg, he sent his right elbow down towards her knee.

Using his hold on her as he hooked her leg she dropped down landing on her back she swiftly kicked out and twisted so her other leg would come across to hit his elbow knocking it away from her. At the same time cause him to release her she would end in a crouching position looking at him.

Continuing to smirk as he looks down at her, grabbing her hair in a tight, and rough grip he swung his knee directly towards her face.

Fearil brought her hands up blocking the blow pushing his knee to the side so it would go past her face. Turning her head to the side his grip on her hair hurt like hell but she was determined.

she reached between his legs hooked her arm around his knee and threw as much of her weight and body into it as she could to trip him. Takeing him to the ground he would let go of her hair or rip some of it out in the process.

Ether way her eyes reflected the pain but she ignored it and scrambled over him.. drawing what energy she qucikly could.

"yer mine now " she brought her hand up intending to kill him by forcing air into him which would cause his lungs to explode but something stopped her ...she frowned not understanding her hesitation.

With that same smirk he brough his legs up, hooking under her arms, and over her shoulder, forcing her onto her back and making him sit up in the process. Looking down at her he sent a right hook to her jaw to knock her out of it.

as his fist hit Faeril was out for the count at least for the time being.

"Not bad " With another shake of his head he uncoiled his legs from her, and slowly kneeled next to her looking down at her, he began feeling all the damage to himself but using his hands checked her over as well making sure she remained knocked out.

Faeril remained unconsious through out his examintation, but she wouldnt be out for long.

He kisses her cheek softly, the maze and the seal vanishing just as quickly as they appeared before he sheathed his blades and got dressed and had to admit even if only to himself she was lovely however she was trying to kill him.

Faeril frowned even unconsios as he kissed her cheek as if confused a low groan escaping giving indication she would be waking.

Using what little time he had left, he carefully gathered her weapons and piled them together away from her.

....

Shaemus sat there laying on his stomach on a small rock which happened to be floating above the site of their battle, he rested his chin in the palms of his hands as he watched the fight, it was very pretty, though not in the usual sense of beauty. While others could see just the flash and flow of sword and blood, he saw a need, both combatants had a greed so hightened that their auras were leaving trails of gold like streamers made of cloud and mist.

This would be how shaemus followed Faeril, he had followed the golden trail she left behind, the scent of greed which not only permiated the air as she passed, but stained the surrounding vegetation with a shade of gold and glimmer only the eyes of a leprechuan or other fey creature could see.

Durring the fighting tho she couldnt remember when the cloth she had had over her face had come away.. she was waking taking inventory. Her body ached from head to toe especally her ribs but thos would heal before long..nothing seemed broken she was suprised frankly that she was alive.

slowly she opened her eyes and sat up she took a sharp indrawn breath as the motion hurt she spoted him instantly, and igrnoring her protesting ribs swiftly got to her feet.

Auto maticly reaching for her wepons she smiled as she spotted them well away from her she slowly relaxed.." why didna ye kill me ?"

Smiling softly he seemed different, lighter and more friendly as he looks at her standing up, dusting himself off by patting down his clothes. he shurgged and stated " That wouldn't be right killing family"

"Family ? how in bloody hell are ye family !?"

"My name is Jarel Druidoak im your adopted brother so to speak my mother was a full blooded Lycon and my father unknown yours found me and took me in.."

"i supose sence ye introduced yerself i must needs do so as well.. dunna think i ha fergiven ye yet... but i supose tis only right fer ye ta know whos tryin ta kill ye..."

"i be Faeril.. an i ha know idea wha in bloody hell yer talkin abou as i dunna ken who these Druidoaks be. Tho ye claim me da adopted ye. Yer out o luck there fer i dunna remember him ether.."

He looked at her a moment assessingly and reolized she hunted him for the loss of her crew and not for the many other reasons she should be. Wynwillow didnt remember who she truly was..

Jarel smiles as he sits back down cross legged. appearing thoughtful and contemplative it would be fun toying with her." Father was an old fellow and gatherd a group of us known as the DarkOaks pitty you tracked us down and was convinced we were up to no good and he couldnt perswade you to join us."

Faeril frowned not sure what to make of his words she was letting herself get distracted however even sitting cross legged as he was she had a feeling if she went for her wepons he was fast enough to block her..

"Observation and perseption, for example. You want to go for you're weapons but you know due my control over light i can move faster than you and most probably end you if i wished."

she tilted her head listining a slow grin spreading across her feature she saw no reason to deny his statment of fact " aye tho i had ye fer a wee while dunna ge too cocky lad.."

"A battle is won through more than just weapons and power and skill. You require a very keen eye to keep an eye on your opponents. Perception to anticipate their actions before they do"

Faeril rolled her eyes but if he wanted a debate and to lecture her who was she to complain boring yes, but it wouldnt kill her. "i dunna thin i did tha badly... i had no intneded ta engage ye as o yet. mearly watch ye an learn what i could first.. knowing ones oponant before facin them if one is able is a wise corse"

"Correct however, what you didn't realise is while you were watching me, the shadows were watching you. I was watching you while you were watching me, if i wanted i could of had the shadows launch a surprise attack."

He noted her rolled eyes and wasnt sure if he wanted to throttle her again or maybe kiss her something about her. Focus your goal in the end is to kill her, and well the more you learn the easer that will be she did nearly have you he thought, and he could have finnsihed his goal but he admired her skill.

“aye tis why i tought ta retreate an regroup there are vera few things i could thin of ta imprison let alone actually attack ye an nether o which i ha on me a the time.”

“To imprison me would be to imprison both light and darkness itself”

“aye i am aware”

“And how do you imprison both of them without leaving one behind for me to use”

“tha be fer me ta discover an ye ta find out”

Jarel laughs and smirks as he winks at her and slowly stands up, dusting off his trousers again. There was no possable way she could defeat him in the end he would have her. There was no rush he would delight in coming at her again another time and again until he got board. He yawns as he starts to walk away from her, waving behind him as he does.

Faeril watched him go waiting listinging she made no move twords her weopons simply thought over things he had said.

A flash of white light burst forth in an instant from Jarel and just as instantaniously as it appeared, it disappeared and Jarel was gone.

when he was gone and she could detect no trace of his scent any longer only then did she move twords her wepons and placed them back where they belonged she knew they would meet again

Faeril once all her things had been gathered left the area swiftly using the wind wraping it around her to help cover her tracks, and hide her scent she had a few other tricks up her sleeves as well but what troubled her was.. why had she hesitated when she had him.

she searched that realm for weeks after before returning to her new crew to try a different realm and to seek out some crystals she had heard of from a crew member. That just might be of use against Jarel if they cross paths again it was a risky move but if it worked.. she grinned then twould be she who held the upper hand.

Chapter 10

Having woke up feeling hungry for the taste of the Tavern food. He flew there thinking of the taste of the food they wernt on earth but in another regon a few months travel from ether Easur or Earth. his mouth was watering as he entered the tavern.

wearing his usual garb of vest shirt, pants and boots, momentarily he stops as he closes the door taking in all around. He believes he recognizes one however he stays quiet and the other not sure of. He makes his way to the counter, sits and orders breakfast with fresh milk*

there was a roudy group inside the tavern rasing tankerds laughing and cheering there captin conversing about a susessful raid.. singing a durnken balled of one sort or another there captin raising her own tankered and downing it.

she looked very much like Wynwillow save her clothing and jewlery was different she also held a scar on her temple coming from the top of her for head down to just above her eye.

her first mate held burn scars on his arms hands and back from having gotten her out of the cave after it exploded both of them the only survivors he had hidden her and gotten them both away he remembered everthing but knew she remembered nothing.

While ordering Vukan notices the rowdy group laughing, singing, and having a good time. It was the captain that caught his attention. He could not believe his eyes. she looked like his love Wynwillow.

However he is not sure. Her scent is somewhat masked or he forgot how he could forget however was beyond him as close as he and wyn had been becoming before he had gone to spend time with his sister and vaul... No he would never forget her scent.

He is perplexed ... he takes in a deeper breath and holds it, eyes closed, making his senses remember. He turns so as not to draw attention to himself as he waits for his food. It couldnt be her could it. He had just received word through the crystal Rhannon had given him that Wyn had been killed in an explosion of some kind.

Faeril's back had been turned it wasnt until she slapped one of her crewmen upon his back turning with him that she noticed the other sitting at the bar eating. something about him seemed familiar to her her pink colored eyes moved over his form the way his mucles played beneath his shirt the way his wings moved up and down with each breath.

something about him captured her interest nagging at the back of her mind that they had met her eyes narrowed and she looked much more serious as she studied him further then shook her head of her thoughts as her head begain to hurt.

Her injuries from the fight with Jarel had been healed by her first mate once she had made it back to ship, and theyed come here to give the men some much needed shore leave before setting out once more.

a hand moved to her forhead where the scar on her temple resided she rubbed it absently then turned to the crewmen who spoke to her " Come captin its been a long evening let the crew have there fun and shore leave for the night i'll mix the powders for your head " Faeril grinned and shoved him off shaking her head. " Nay i'll ha none o tha nasty stuff ye say will aid me.. tis not a good tankered o rum will na cure.."

Turning in his seat, Vukan decides to watch the one called 'captain'. Somewhere in the back of his mind his sense of smell assures him it is her however just barely.

Knowing him self, just that small amount of possibility is enough for him to openly watch regardless of consequenses. He watches as she moves, as she speaks, notices she is drinking rum. a favorite of Wyns if he remembers correctly.

He over hears one asking her to go so he can fix powders for her. He thinks 'Powders' what sort of stuff is she taking? The crew appear to be hers as they are having a good time and no one is actually forcing her nor does she appear to be watched over.

Curious he decides to approach to see what happens. He gets up from his stool at the counter and walks straight up to the one called 'Captain' placinng a hand on her shoulder he also emits a small lightning charge, as if static electricity, to see how she reacts as he steps back once he makes contact.

The crew as Vukan made his way closer to there captin each grew quiet and more attentive not quite as in there cups yet as one would supose each drawing there weopns as his hand touched her sholder.

The captin had been aware of his growing closeness as his scent had grown stronger as soon as his hand made conact she reached up took hold of it gasping slighty at the shock, but ignoring it.

She kept hold of the hand ducking under it. turning moving behind him brining his arms with her so that she and it were now behind his back she moved swiftly with nearly bluring speed inteding to pin him up against the wall.

The sudden swiftness of her impressed him as she took his arm and moved behind him, he could feel she wanted to move him so he went with the flow for now. He was smiling and chuckling a bit, as she stood he was able to see her eyes.

There was no mistaking those pink eyes. He has never seen others like them. This is Wyn he was certain of it. His heart did a dance. As she pinned him to the wall in a warm inviting voice he said. " Welcome Back Wynwillow it has been a while since I last smelled you and saw those beautiful pink eyes of yours. " He waits for her response never once attempting to fight her grip or her.

She frowned as he allowed her to pin him her crew clamoring for her to finnsih him for daring to lay a hand on her kept her hold on his arm with one hand and raised her other to silence her crew.

instantly they obayed the signal a small smerk played acorss her lips her pink colored eyes met thos colbolt blue his scent drawn into her lungs eyes narrowed and focused tho showing some hint of pain she was hiding

"i think lad ye've me confused wi another i've no idea who this Wynwillow is ye seek but i bet shes a bonnie lass if ye say she looks anythin like me.. " slowly she eases back letting him go.

stepping back amongst her crew she crossed her arms waiting for him to turn around " yer wyn be a lucky lass ta ha one such as ye lookin fer her.. tis a shame i'm no her i wouldna refuse ye me bed.."

As she grinned her crew new she wouldnt let them hurt him unless he did something foolish and so resheathed there wepons only one the one with burns watched them closely as they talked

Turning he looks over to see who is watching as he heard all weapons come out. It appeared only the one with the burns seemed intent on what happens. As he turns his gaze to hers, taking in those pink eyes.

He takes a step forward bringing himself within a breathes length in front of her. He smiled knowing she would show no give nor back down in front of her crew.

While he was taller than she, he placed his hands at his side, and bent forward with deliberate slowness for all to see. As his head settled alongside hers.

he drew a deep breath taking her scent into him savoring every second of it as a full dose confirmed it was she. With his lips very close to her ear he whispers for only her to hear

"I would take you up on your offer for bed however I would prefer you being you. The one I seek is listening to my voice at this very moment, only she cant hear me. I know not what name you go by but to me you are Wynwillow and shall always be. I am Vukan of Firelight. We met on a beach as well as at WhiteOak and you invited me to join you at a wedding ..... take your time remembering."

Noticing a wince on her face as he speaks he trys not to show too much concern for it would be seen as a weakness and hed lose her interest. "if you are injured I would be happy to heal you. Take a moment and think, Wynwillow, look around all of this is already you."

He was pushing things he knew it he didnt know what was wrong wether she was pretending to be someone else for a reason or if she truly didnt remember. taking a risk knowing it will be his head, with blurring speed he places his hands on her shoulders and his lips on hers kissing her with a long lost passion only if he catches her off guard

some of the crew tensed and watched waiting few dared approch there captin let alone were bold enough to kiss her infront of her crew no less.. some cheered his boldness others prepaired for a fight all watching. Each placing bets and taking odds on the outcome.

Faeril's head did indeed hurt more and more as he spoke immages starting to crowed in on her her heart rate picked up a small spark of hope, and larger one of desire ignighiting with in her.

Questions she had asked herself time and again forming in her mind why coulnt she remember anything from before a few months ago.. before she could respond to his statements he was kissing her.

Her hands came up between them sliding up his chest to rest momentairly on his sholders she knew she should pull away, but his touch, scent, and feel were mesmerizing .she could feel the warmth and strenght of his body threw there clothing.

It had her reeling and nearly week kneed it was that last that recovered her wits somewhat her hands grabbed hold of his vest and she dropped down to her back bringing her feet up into him intending to flip him up and over her.

At this point Shaemus who had been discovering this taverns version of rum and the complexities of the flavors hidden within while sitting in the rafters of the tavern was startled by the sudden comotion of the tussle begining below him, "that pink eyed flea bag sure likes ta fight doesn't she?"

....

Hibiki the male was an anomality as far as most creatures go only he truly knew his origins and very few were able to get him to talk, though he was able to communicate even without speaking much.

his eyes were that of an unnatural glowing violet hue his pupils were that of crossed slits he had no weaponry on him and had a black under shirt that was sleeveless he seemed to have some sort of strange tattoo like markings that seemed to be covering the young male's entire body.

his pants seemed to be connected to his self made toeless shoes and shirt he had an armored vest that was old and had seen better days the boy looked as if covered in ash smoke dried blood and other debris his hair covered his eyes when he looked down other than that his face was visible for the most part the boy who had been walking through the land he found himself in looked to be twenty years of age and was maybe human or elf by looks but by scent he was something else entirely something that was unknown the male was in all honesty twelve years of age and had been looking for a safe place to rest from training and to clean his filth.

He had spotted the castle that he was rather close to he looked down at his filthy form then shook his head silently thinking to himself 'there is no way that I would even be greeted there even if I was clean I don't even truly know who I am.. I gave myself my name even…

tch.. better move on before im spotted and thought of as a thief or worse' after he shook his thinking from his head he had stopped walking for a moment to allow his legs a moment to rest then started to walk to where he thought he heard running water.

unknown to him however his worries of guards or other such was misplaced as the castle was abandoned due to attacks on it still he was more cautious due to the recent events that had taken place he then thought siently to himself 'wait a minute… why go this far for someone like me? Im human aren't i? no that cant be…

demons and vampires wouldn't do all this just for a human. So not only do I not know who I am and have no given name besides ultra violet devil because of my eyes I know not even what I am… this leaves too many questions for me to answer.

Damn it! Im only twelve years old!' he then would continue his walk twords the river which was a corpse drop location but this was unknown to Hibiki as he could not smell over the filth that covered him

Honnora having heard roomers on earth from adewen about other demons left Riaden in charge of WhiteOak off and on to go and investagate as Adewen wasnt fully recovered yet from healing the Dragon wolfen who had come to her for aid..

Honnora came instead.. Idri was about 5 years old now Greystone had taken Idri to earth to visit Donovan his mate Destiny and grandson Neko who Idri enjoyed spending time with..

it was night as she flew low weving in and out among the trees following some unsuhual scents she wasnt familar with landing she took on the form of what the humans called a fox and padded closer to the castle ahead.

by the time the male had come across the multitude of corpses that lay near the river Hibiki let out a light groan his voice sounded like that of a pure celestial shaking his head at the pile of rotting corpses.

He started to walk up river to try and find a clean spot only to learn that the water was toxic by something he couldnt figure out he let out a light sigh and slumped down against a tree resting as he wasnt sure how long it would have been before his legs gave out from exhaustion

something aside from the smell of rotten corpses caught her attention what ever it was it reaked she moved therw the under bursh getting closer watching quietly

the 'tattooed' male who looked no more than a child would have been seen by the 'fox' covered in ash black smoke blood gore and sut and had been seen resting against a tree near the large toxic lake the boy's haiir had been matted to his skin by blood and shreded organs and other such gore though none of the blood was his own..

....

Vuken heard noise in the background but paid it no heed This one before him held his full attention. To feel her lips on his, her scent wafting about him, her hands as they came to rest on his shoulders how he has wanted to feel these for so long.

Before he lost what thinking he had he remembered she is battle tested and worthy of full attention. Knowing she is having some sort of memory issue he feels her arms tense as she grabs his vest quickly recognizing she is going to do something.

As she drops to her back, he anticipates she is going to try and throw him. As she drops down attempting to keep him up so she can get her legs under him, Vukan drops with her willingly and brings up his right knee wedging between her legs not letting her get them under him.

as he falls on top of her from the waist down, keeping his arms outward just to the edges of her body so he uses the floor not her to keep himself from crushing her. Intensely looking into her dazzling pink eyes damn why can he not think of anything but thos eyes " May we talk as I buy you some rum?"

she gazed up at him the tension in the air from her crew as they waited to hear wether she would order them to haul him off and pummle him or aceept his offer they hadnt seen anyone outsmart her as he had just done.

Of course shaemus was not surprised that he had outsmarted her but was still watching intently to see how she would deal with this upstart, especially since his tankard was dry.

they visably releaxed as she laughed one of her hands going to the back of his head as she leaned up and kissed him her body becoming inflamed a wildness of need rising inside of her demanding.

they visably releaxed as she laughed one of her hands going to the back of his head as she leaned up and kissed him her body becoming inflamed a wildness of need rising inside of her demanding.

nibbling at his lips and deepining the kiss between them before gentling it drawing back her hunger and need tho lingering turned gental as she let him go to speak " Aye lad ye ken buy me a round er two..."

The other didnt like what he was seeing and was angry but she was captin and he even had he been in charge one thing remained the same as ever nothing budged the captin unless she willed it.." me name is Faeril by the by an im vera pleased ta meet ye Vukan.. now then are ye gonna let me up er do i ha ta move ye ?"

Never taking his eyes off of hers as she kissed him his desire shot off like the flames of a forge as the fires are lit.. he kissed her back with longing, yearning, needing to have like never before. Somewhat surprised by his inabliity to control his bodies reaction yet at same time very happy for it.

When she breaks the kiss introducing herself and accepting his drink offer he smiles " I would prefer a moment to get myself under control before I get up. Actually I should be alright for the moment until I rethink your offer of going to bed"

he smiles and chuckles as he gets up to his feet bending he offers her his hand to help her up." Hopefully my breakfast is served and I will get you your drink, rum if I heard correctly. " He moves back to his seat at the counter.

she grinned accepting his hand and moved with him to the bar one of her other crew slapping the man with the burnt hands on the back laughingly saying. " looks as if the captins found someone ta enjoy the evenin with. ye shoul considr doin the same"

the man with the burn hands eyes glittered dangerously and he playfully punched his companion back then nodded and grinned moving to do just that finding one of the taverns wenches " aye rum tis.. sa then lad tell me o yer self "Faeril stated as she sat next to him.

Vukan waits till she sits before sitting, not because she is the captain but because she is a lady. After she sits, he smiles at her question and retorts. " I will gladly tell you of myself but first, you will have to tell me about the one with the burns."

"He looked none the happy about how I spoke nor what I did and the glint in his eye tells me I should watch my back. So what is his story and how is he so protective of you? Wait " he puts up a hand as the thoughts keep rolling within him.

“My thoughts are racing away from me. Before I listen to anything, Faeril, may I attempt to heal or help with what causes you pain?”

Faeril looked at him skepticly.. wondering why he was so blasted curious “ now why then would i be allowin ye ta do such when we just met ? “ her eyes glitter with a hint of mischevous humor considering he had kissed her and she him.. she ignored his other questions for the time being “ if i were ta allow such how would ye go about it ?”

....

a few moments had passed with the boy resting there before heavy footsteps could be heard near the body pile down river of the voices was rather dark and menicing “you STILL havent found it yet? FIND IT NOW!! otherwise its you i will start my testing on you putrid filled walking corpse”

after the deep male voice was finished barking orders scrambling would have been heard as the other presences vanish the seeming to be leader grumbled angrily “ugh all this just to capture a single brat that doesnt eve know what it is... i dont have any information and the scent of death is too strong here to smell the brat out time to search the next area to see if i cant rid myself of this vile stench..”

after this would be said the rest of the footsteps would be heard walking away although the boy had smirked inwardly losing his persuers he remained completely still resting as much as he could while looking and smelling like one of the corpses they had placed.

he had thought it was a clever idea though he was already covered in the gore and dried blood after he was sure that they had left his glowing violet eyes with cross slit pupils began to slowly open and the male’s eyes started to sca the area falling on the ‘fox’ that was ear him he only made a gesture to the animal to stay low and quiet not knowing what or who the fox truly was

the fox’s tail curled round it as it got to its feet but remained crouched low ready to run or attack which ever the case may be as the voices and other beings drew nearer her ears were flat against her head she remained utterly still until they had gone.

then looked over at the boy seeing him motion for her to remain low and quite her ears came up and head tilted questioningly before nodding as if saying i understand with out words and waited ears turning this way and that listinging as well as sniffing the air

now hearing total silence he only needed to do two things keep from being spotted untill day break and find a reletively safe place to hide untill they thought he was dead his eyes narrowed as he knew that he would have to wait.

about three more hours before he could move about freely although even longer before he could wash the filth from himself the vampires who were searching for him had moved completely from the forest and were searching the next area.

the boy had let out a silent sigh of releif as he could now rest somewhat easier but knew better than that he had quietly moved to a corpse and taken a dagger from it sliding it into his armor to give the appearence that he was just another that had been killed in senseless battle.

as he laid there he closed his eyes but was paying full attention to his suroundings while concealing every bit of his presence unless he was seen he could not be detected he rested there for the next two hours before the sun had started to creep over the mountian tops causing vampires to head to darker places

the fox slowly crept out of her hidding spot as the boy moved to gather the dagger from the corpse she looked in the direction the vampires had gone then back to him debating wether to stay with him or track the vampires.

it was unushal she thought to see so many together wernt they ushually solitary creatures this confirmed some of the tales ade had heard and passed on but she had yet to see any demons connected with them.

secondly Wyn had been missing for over a year now she dared not let herself get distracted too much she would worrie for wyn another day. Looking back to the boy she nodded to him as if saying thanks and good luck all at once before moving swiftly threw the undergowth to track the vampires and see where they would lead.

the youg boy nodded and slowly started to move before freezing in place as another demon in human form started to look over at the fox then grumble as it walked away "how in the abyss did we lose a kid that was in the village.. we need to find him to bring him back to the labs, damn fox was sniffing the body pile..." as the being walked away the boy gritted his teeth as that encounter was too damn close for comfort

....

Within Vukans cobalt blue eyes flashes of lightning could be seen or sparkles depending on how one would describe it.. " First of all you have already started it by kissing me and I you. " he stops his discription and shakes head laughing.

"Actually we could do it here and now " I would face you and you me. I would place my hands on the side of your head and concentrate my energies to you. Depending on what is injured depends on how long it may take. I see you have a scar on your head, you feel fine right now I'm sure so all I could do is try. What is most bothering you?"

"hmmm i rather like yer first suggestion .. would ye consider joinin me crew comin wi us wi me perhaps ?.. hower i thin yer second suggestion would be best. till be a test in trust an i 'll no ha any aroun me i dunna trust.. occasionally me head troubles me but no often."

"least wise till no of late certin scents an sounds trigger memories i canna focus on which causes the pain.. some thin abut it places an aye people seem familar, but i canna place them.. ye asked after me first mate.."

she looked over to him. “Lochlen sr. be his name i dunna remember what happend only tha we were in an explosion o some sort tis how he were burnt an i gained this as well as other wounds”

“Faeril, as you call yourself, there are two ways we can go about this. I shall let you decide how you would like to do this. One way is and I’m pretty sure your body will respond, we share energy you allowing me to find the physcial wrongs, and tend to them correcting or fixing them, such as minimizing the scar, it will not go away but it will be barely visible.”

He held up a hand silently asking her to allow him to continue with out interupting. Suprised she was being as forth coming and co opritive as she was he was guessing she felt some connection and didnt know why herself.

“Second is we do the first along with allowing me to access your memories and you mine to help make a connection to what you cannot do, but plagues you constantly. This second way may take time and more than one try.”

“There are things we will see about each other that no one else has ever seen. I have done something like this once before therefore it will take a few times. I was successful but they were willing and I was also. The sharing can be very intimate. The choice is yours.”

“Oh also, I overheard something about powders, you will have to stop taking whatever that is. I already know it is part of the problem. Take your time to think”

His food arrived along with her rum, he turns and devours the meal in front of him one to keep from staring at the beautiful woman she is, second he wants to kiss her again, third he needs to let her have time to think.

“i dunna ken why but yer words sound true ta me “ looks thoughtful as well as serious “ there be risk in ether perposal ye suggest hower i’ll ether remember er i willna. ye are aright about the powders i dunna care fer them hower they ha eased the pain in me head in past."

"if yer sucess ful twill no longer be needed.. an as id love ta share me body wi ye i see no harm in sharen wi ye me mind given i dunna ken me past if it helps sa be it an all the mur fun fer the both o us should we be sharen each other as well"

a hand with a tankerd in it came down between them the hand was burned the male moving closer seperating them as Vukan ate. "Captin i must protest you know nothing of this fellow how can you accept him so easly and readly ?"

Faerl kicked the males legs from under him grabbing the back of his head she slamed it against he bar counter and let him fall to his knees. she stood and kicked him in the face watching him fall back wards looking up at her with his nose bleeding.

Lachlen didnt move just lay there as she placed a foot on his chest the rest of the crew some passed out from drink others already having disapeared with a wench or two.. ones that were still awake shaking there heads others grinning

"First off I be captin an i'll be damned if ill have ye call me judgement inta question.. secondly no tha i ha ta answer ta ye Lachlen er any other.. he'll be comin wi us so's i can ge ta know him better .. much much better an quite intamatly.. should he so choose. if ye dunna like it ye ken find another burth an captin ta sale under me personal affairs are me own... am i clear ?.."

he nodded " i canna hear ye..." Lachlen spoke then " Aye i hear an obey captin.." Wyn/Faeril removed her foot from his chest he got up and gave Vukan a look then turned to leave the tavern

Never missing a beat of eating Vukan watched from the corner of his vision and completed eating making sure he watched as the one called Lachlen got to his feet and gave his look.

Without hesitation tossing his empty plate to the counter her pushed away from the counter standing and within 4 steps he took, branches of wood wrapped around the ankles of Lachlen holding him in place, allowing him to get more pissed, Vukan turned to Faeril " May I have a moment with him, my Lady?"

Faeril looked at him impressed with his skill and grinned finding it funny his calling her Lady. " short o killin him he be yers. kill him an answer ta me. he is unless he choses otherwise still a member o me crew"

Vukan gets up and walks over to Lachlen, getting right in front of him close enough that his and Lachlen noses are about an inch apart, looking him in his eyes with a very blank look on Vukans face very neutral.

He lets the branches disengage from the ankles. " I believe it best we not get off on the wrong side of the bed in this matter. You appear to have a bit more affection for your captain than a loyal crew member. I would also guess you are medically inclined and possibly second in command on board? Am I close? " still with a neutral look on his face and very easy deep voice.

Lachlen simply nodded if he were greatful for being released didnt show it simply widened his stance crossing his arms over his chest. He kept his voice low so it wouldnt carrie not wanting the captin or the crew what was left of those not passed out to hear the conversation.

He met vukans eyes and smerked.." what is it to you.. you wont last you'll get what you want of her and then be gone..or she you " he was angry and he knew the captin better than that he knew she was the type that where her body went eventually so too would her heart.

she had never given in to any others nor appeared attracted to any till now but he hoped if vukan thought he was one of many fleeting in and out that he wouldnt stay at least that was his thinking in th matter

not changing any facial features except the lightning seen in his eyes. the only thing seen was by Lachlen. Vukan can sense the anger from him, and jealous from him regarding her.

Taking a moment never letting his eyes wonder from Lachlen he answered " To me it is everything and nothing. You have a job she expects of you do it and leave medical things to me for now."

lowering his voice even more just above a whisper so only Lachlen can hear. "Lachlen we both will be watching the other from this point forward, this I know. You do your job and I will do what I do."

"Neither knows where this is going so let us enjoy the journey or we may find the end can be deadly. " Vukan extends a hand and steps back " It has been a pleasure Lachlen, I look forward to many more intimate moments down the road to share with you. " Vukan smiles waiting for his reaction

Lachlen pasted on a false smile and nodded takeing vukans hand he then walked past him and to return to the ship with out another word. Faeril walked up next to Vukan looking up at him. "well then seems hell no be givin ye an easy time o it sure ye still wish ta join me an me crew vukan ?"

I would have it no other way he thought fearcly. " yes I will join you if only to keep an eye on you myself as well as your second. " turning to her. " which in case, I will kill if he messes with you in a manner I find unsuitable for a captain, a lady and Damarian."

"Answering to you will be a pleasure if I must. " keeps voice low as he doesn't want to cause issue in front of her crew. " When do you set out again? do I have time to gather things and say goodbyes?"

"aye ye have time we leave in two days time me crew deserved a rest after our last voyage an dose he deserve his fate then ill no stop ye from deliverin it ta him."

"should i be no capabale o doin so meself.. hower keep in mind should ye oer step till be ye whos fed ta the sharks." she had grinned over his causing her a lady thinking it a humorus as it wasnt a title she remembered being applyed to her and was a bit puzzled about the damarian refrance.

Faeril motioned for him to lead the way out of the tavern to his own quarters with in the village as they continued the conversations.

"Two days uh? I can deal with that. What shall I bring for this next voyage? allow me to help with the pain in your head. I will place my hands on the side of your face put yours on top of mine and relax. Think whatever you want just relax. I will attempt to clear up the pain physically and if I wonder anywhere I shouldn't just say so I will move on."

Seeing the look in her pink eyes he quickly states "No I will not intentionally do anything unless you say ok just when sharing things sometimes happen. ok, ready?"

The tavern behind them they continued on there conversation drifting away from the ears of those inside.

Shaemus, already bored from the interactions of the captain and her guest as they slipped outside of the tavern, slumped against the rafter, "and she seemed to be such a fireball before",

he smiled as he dug into his pocket and produced a piece of fool's gold the size of his fist, he blew on it to make it grow to the size of him and polished it up to look like a huge gold nugget, then proceeded to roll it accross the rafters to just over the circle of her crew.

His smile grew as he nudged it off the rafters to have it fall into the burned one's tankerd, flattening it against the table like a paper cup. imediately all eyes around the table drew to the nugget and greed quickly filled those pirate hearts as all lept after it and the fight for the fool's nugget comenced.

with Shaemus looking down wincing as some punches were thrown and some bottles broken over heads, and other moves. he would be throwing punches as if he were in the group fighting them off. And as the uproaor continued no one could hear the chipper chirp of the bellowing leprechuan in the rafters.

Suddenly impatient and feeling playful as he watched her think the matter through he continued distracting her from her thoughts " Are you going to let me get my hands on you Faeril or not? " he smiles his colbolt blue eyes dancing with as much humor as hers as he gazes into them

"imaptient are ye lad.." she grins " aye i'll let ye ge yer hands an mur on me in but a moment er two.. " she chuckles pink colored eyes dancing with humor as she tilts her head back to look up at him.

Her white hair with black tips falling back from her sholders down her back the chains upon her horns swaying slightly with her movements " if ye wish i'll no stop ye. i were wonderin tho du ye no ha any wepons ?"

Vukan laughed at all she said and then nodded turning he summons his weapon for Faeril to see than hides it again a broad sword came to his hand from a rift in the ground that opened when he summoned it he held it in his hands for her to see before opening the rift once again and sending the sword back to wence it came. " I have other swords but this is always with me."

Faeril watched as Vukan summoned the wepon crossing her arms over her chest she studied it before he made it vanish once more she looked over to another fellow who drew his sword as well and smiled. " are ye offerin ta join me crew as well ?

she teased a bit as Vukan spoke to him reasuring the male all was well ..however she had drawn one of her daggers silently her action hidden by the way she and Vukan were standing when the male eased back down passafied by Vukans explinations as they talked over wepons she just as quietly resheathed it..

Vukan turned back to Wyn or rather Faeril smiling at her he gently cupped her head in his hands closing his eyes he relaxed his hands began to glow with a soft warm light the warmth spread threw wyns body as he begain attempting to heal her.

she staried intently up at him when he turned back to her..her pink colored eyes meeting that of his colbolt blue feeling totally bemused she wondered breifly if he had cast some sort of spell which drew her to him.

He lookd so calm and unruffled and yet there was a sense of power as well she closed her eyes as his energy moved from him into herself and begain the healing process unaware of the passage of time as he was able to lesson the pain pounding in her head.. Her hands lightly came up to rest on his arms over his elbows with out consious thought.

Of the injurie itself tho there would reamin a faint scar it was not as prominent as it had been she opened her eyes looking at him again as the warm feeling faded and his hands stopped glowing he opened his eyes and asked " how do you feel now ?"

a soft smile plays about her lips her hands slid from his elbows up to his hands tracing a gental pattern along his wrists before letting out a breath having to force herself to think about the question itself and his meaning her injurie vurses the termoil of the growing storm inside her caused simply by being near him " aye much better ye ar indeed a merical worker"

Vukan begain chuckling at her words " Nay I am not a miracle worker, just one who has learned to heal as all Damarians can. " Looks at her wondering just how much he should push right now.

"just as you can also did you not feel the energy? You are a Damarian and when we get your memories flowing correctly you will know. " he pauses noticeing the quizzical look on her face. " No I am not magical nor have I done anything to you."

"We are familiar to one another, you can sense that, it is what allows us to talk as if ... we have done before. I will admit I am taking advantage by kissing you, but it is what I was going to do the next time I saw you.

Regardless of who you think you are or know you are, I was kissing those lips of yours while looking into such beautiful pink eyes."

he stops takes a moment knowing hes probably over doing it and making a mess of things he was suprised she hadnt kicked him in the face or told him to screw off. " I have time tell me where we are going on this next trip?"

Faeril grinned slid her hand up his chest then lifted it to brush some of the strey blue black locks from his eyes so she could see them clearly. lost in there depths for the moment before recalling there surroundings.

She was tempted to take his hand and drag him off to her ship and the privacy of her cabin " i dunna ken much o anythin past a few months ago as ta where we be goin " she shrugs " im a pirate lad an i'll no be revealin such thins here in the open"

Vukan found himself chuckling and smiling again a near perminent state around her that he found he enjoyed emensly " I guess you wouldn't do that. Allow me to change my question. how long do you suspect we will be away from here? From this realm from Earth and from Easur?"

"ahhh now tha be a different tale indeed a fortnight may hap two dependin on how all fairs"

with the movements of her hands and how she is looking at him Vukan is of the notion to grab her and take her home to his bed. He has dreamt of her since that first moment on the beach.

He knows waiting a bit more till she is herself completely is the least he could do but by the gods he knows he will break before then. her pull, her aura, her presence sets him into that primal state.

she saw much tho she suspected like most males wouldnt like that she was reading him so well she saw an intense hunger and balent desire that sparked an answering heat within her own soul his voice and wary grin as he chuckled was sinfully delightful to listen to.

How she wondered would she guard her heart from thos intense eyes and perfectly tempting mouth a sweep of color rose to her cheeks and she blushed she pulled a way trying to hide her suprise she never blushed what was wrong with her.. she wondered if she were becoming ill

Faeril tilted her head back a bit to look at him fully once more they were close enough she could kiss him or he her easly why she hesitated she had no earthly idea.

she was pirate and used to these last months simply taking what she wanted so why didnt she it was clear she wanted him and he her " ye ken call me wyn all ye like lad but dunna mistake the person i am here an now fer the one ye thin i am er was.."

she cautioned him " as ye saw wi Lochlen i ha a temper an will act swiftly when i feel the need best be thinkin o that an compairin tha ta what plesures ye may find in me bed. an thin long an hard wether ye wish ta take the risk.. i'll brook no insabordnation an fer yer sake part o me hopes i am who ye say else yer in fer much disapoint ment down the road"

Not taking his eyes from her for a millisecond he listened to all she had to say stepping back to give them both some breathing space. " Wyn, whether you are like you are now or revert back to who I once knew you as or change completely. Deep inside you is the one i know and will learn to love."

"Perhaps I am not as timid as I may appear here, while I will go with you, I go as a consultanlt and will stand my own ground. I will not disrespect you or try to take your ship or crew. I will be me. if I find myself in your bed it will be for pleasure and company not to be your captain or take your ship."

"As for your temper if you think that bothers me mayhaps you should think back as I never stopped my pace of eating while you did what you felt you needed to. I will defend myself at all times so if you feel the need to flash your anger don't be startled if I flash back. I believe we understand each other now don't we?"

she laughed then her eyes dancing with acceptance and delight " aye lad i beleive we ha an accord now the only question remains will ye be joinin me this night er returnin ta yer kin afore we both lose our heads in what sparks be flyin between us an say yer fairwells"

she once again felt the heat of his body so close to hers as his arm went round her and he kissed her his mouth fastioned to hers sweeping them both away to lofty hights a current seemed to flow between them.

a sensual promise that hightned as she moved closer molding her body to his her arms sliding up around his neck one hand in his hair the other resting across his sholders at the base of his neck holding him to her her soft curves fitting agaisnt the mucles of his body starining for his touch nether rememberd how they got from the tavern to his home that night only they had arrived safely.

Faeril streached lazly upon Vukans bed a slow satisfied grin upon her lips as she was fully aware of him next to her having made love to him threw out the reamainder of the night and explored every inch of him she turned on her side to face him now watching him sleep he truly was a bonnie mon and was thrilled that he would be coming with her abord ship.

she studied him his bone structure was good high cheek bones a strong jaw he was broad of sholder lean of hip and had long well formed legs his clothing breeches and such did little to hide the strenght in his body.

There was also an elegent handsomeness but it was his eyes when they were open that captured her attention further such a brillant blue she resisted the urge to brush his blue and balck hair back from his face to see more.

Slowly she arose form the bed watching him sleep still then dressed she didnt wake him she let him be. Left his room and home to check on repairs that needed made to the ship and to switch out the crew.

She slipped out of the chamber letting him sleep smiling because she had worn him out truth be told he had worn her out just as much and she didnt want to move however she had a ship to run and a crew to keep in order she left him a note upon his desk after dressing..

Dear Vukan i ha enjoyed last night vera much an look forward ta seen ye again when ye mannage ta arise from yer bed. Come ta this address one o me men will meet ye there an brin ye on ta the ship from there.. ...yers Faeril.

Faeril waited until the next day for Vukan to arrive but he didnt show she was a bit disapointed but such was the life of a pirate she assumed he had simply changed his mind about being with someone of her sort and reputation so turned her attention to the open sea and the adventures that awaited.

Chapter 11

"Evening lady Idrialla" The pride fiend Vaul spoke to the little one as she appeared in his home it was not common for her to come unaccompanied but he supposed she was learning how to get around he would escort her home if Ade did not come soon.

He visited off and on from time to time tho he made sure to pick times when Greystone was not about. He understood Grey s unwillingness to trust tho's outside his own kind but truly such alliances were necessary, he hoped in time the fellow would come around.

"greeting vaul's " Little Idri smiles bounding over to him with youthful enthusiasm "how is yous today's?"

"fairly well young one my thanks for inquiring about such" He smiles and gently pats her head "did you have an eventful day?"

"oh yes's an guess whats two dwagons broughts my guard tos mama ade for her to heals him cas he gots hurted fighting another dwagons it was scarys" Idri still talked of that day in the caverns a year ago as tho it had happened just yesterday.

"I see and is your mother fairing well young one?"

“she wasnts but shes betters nows was awhile agos but me not see you for long long times.. so wanted to tells yous... she passed outs after healings for long times tooks hours an hours cas he was bads offs.”

Storms holdin mama an me in his arms while dragons an my guard fights another dragons in the caves. Before mama passed outs she gaves orders for Storms to gets me to safetys if needs be an not to get in the middle o the dwagons fights unless they asks for aids. Rhannon cames and so did Greystone’s cas mama sent out SOS signal just to be on safe sides.”

Little idri took a deep breath pausing a moment having imparted all her information in one seemingly never ending fast spoken sentence before finishing with.

“me too little’s to helps against dwagons yets”

“I see but I have no doubt your brave enough to have wanted to help” he smiles warmly glad to hear Deaden was alright tho it was a past event it was clearly still upper most in little idri’s mind. “and I hope your mother feels better soon though I know her to have great tenacity and I’m sure she will be back to full strength in a flash of time”

she gazed up at him admiringly nodding as she listened to him.” mama says it takes lots of energy’s to heals even a littles me cants imaginings healing for over 6 hrs no stop ins”

“indeed healing is a very draining art and your mother shows her great prowess by doing such. would you care to go and take a seat young miss I would enjoy talking and hearing that which you and your mother have been up to of late”

Idri glowed feeling important in being asked to sit down “ pleas yes tan me takes your hands?”

He smiles and holds out his hand to allow her to grab his hand if she wants, and he would wait for her to hold his hand before he very casual stride to the end of the room where a half circles of ornate wooden chairs rested

Taking his hand she walks with him to where he wishes to sit smiling purple and blue gem like eyes dancing merrily as she looked around. " this place bigs but me likes its"

"I thank you for the compliment young one. and which chair would you like to sit in?"

"yous welcomes, an i can chooses weally?" she asked eyes wide at being allowed to choose slowly lets go of his hand and moves to one of the chairs then looks at him to make sure its ok before sitting down

He smiles and nods to assure her she can sit wherever she wishes. smiling back she crawls up in the chair to sit even the little one she was in in size comparison nearly swallowed her.

Vaul chuckled warmly amused at the sit of the nervous young idrialla sitting on an oversized chair as he took his seat upon the largest of the chairs lounging with a groan of comfort "so young one can I have my imps bring you anything to eat or drink or would you like to talk first?"

"yes pwes if it no troubles me is hungry s not ea teds yets"

He wondered why she had not eaten as of yet.. "is there anything in particular that sounds yummy to you young one? My imps are quite good at bringing food to suit any taste"

Idri looked thoughtful.. and tentatively asked " you likes cooked chickens?, mama say me not bigs enough for wines yets but it cold outs so maybe hot cocos?"

He smiles and nods closing his eyes for a moment as his horns faintly glow his mind projecting upon the unintelligent imps within his service dancing to the call of their master like puppets tugged by invisible strings.

They quickly get to work melting butter then mixing it with very finely minced garlic, freshly broken sugar cane, a tiny amount of lemon zest.

as the chicken is taken out and dipped into the spiced butter then coated in flour and powdered cheeses such as Parmasian then set within a old log burning baking over as the imps prepare platter of different drinks such as hot coco, grape and pineapple juice mixed, and peach and apple tea.

The wonderful aroma of the cooking chicken and the different drinks presented was mouth watering assault on little idri's senses and surprisingly she passed up the hot coco one of the tease more pleasing to her nose " may me try's that's ones? " she asks motioning to the apple tea

The fiend his eyes remaining closed as he continues to control the imps like puppets but smiles and nods to let idrialla know it was perfectly fine with him for her to take the drink she wanted to try.

as the rest of the imps continue to watch over the cooking chicken letting the chicken's flaky baked crust and skin would turn a golden light brown before pulling it from the over and setting spiriting the chicken onto two plates quickly moving into the room to give young idrialla and their fiendish master their meal.

little idri sips the tea slowly holding the cup carefully in both hands so as not to drop it a quite mm of satisfaction and enjoyment escaping as she very much likes that the taste of the apple tea is as delicious as it smells

Vaul opens his eyes and takes from the platter the peach flavored tea sipping from it with a smile as the plates of baked chicken are brought out as well as two small tables to hold the plates at the imps lightly sprinkle salt on the chicken and rush off always worried that they might get on their masters mood.

"please do feel free to ask young one if you want anything else. the imps are always happy to fetch whatever I ask of them to get or make" “mm oh nos this be more than plenty thanks yous me twin hard to member manors an not dives in it smells so Sammy it hard not to sniff at airs “ she said while she blushes “ Hows is you an Lila’s doings? “ she asked

“a great example of Adewen’s fine work as a parent than you show such manner young one” He smiles and rips small bite sized pieces of chicken from the whole and tossing it into his mouth smiling as he closed his eyes to savor the pungent meld of flavors before he would wash it down with the peach tea.

“so young one tell me how has life within Esuar been since I last visited? and Lila and i are doing well she is still on Earth helping the Daemons group.”

Idri giggled as he tossed the meat into his mouth “ mama is very goods “ she pauses and eats some chicken waiting until her mouth empty before answering.

“Easur goods Wynn missing no one knows where shes gone’s, but she gone long times me hopes shes oks, Rhannon is tea chin younger ones like mes who wants to learns crafting how to do so’s mama teachings fighting’s and elements.. Honnora teaching readings and writings..”

Idri paused in her youthful rambling to take a drink of her tea. While she did so Vaul spoke up. “I see and I can only imagine your doing extremely well in all three topics”

he smiles and assumes a relaxed long position as he continues to partake in the chicken in bite sized pieces ripped from the whole dipping it occasional in Olive oil and butter sauce to give it an even more pungent taste

she nods grinning “ yeps well accepts elements me still has lots o troubles wif those me accidentally blows stuff ups” "you will certainly master it in no time young one of that I can assure you" He partakes of the last bite of chicken on his plate and washes it down with the tea "and I'm gladdened to hear Esuar, and your mother are well has there been anything particularly interesting happening lately?"

Idri shook her head no " not that me can thinks of asides Wyn missing an wolfen get tin hurts an all the dwagons if they were not fighting me would loves to have seen them closer " she said her voice and features holding a hint of wonder.

"ahh so your fascinated in dragons are you young one? i shall keep that in mind should I ever have a chance to send a gift to you and your mother"

"yes me wakes dwagons lots wolfen me guard is a black dwagons he offered to be me guard after i was borne.. he tell me he meet me gamma idrialla long long time agos an owed her a debts.. but he also likes mama an me lots an lots.."

"I see' Vaul stated listening to her.

"at least i think so's sometimes i gets things mixed ups.. mama says me smarts for me age"

"Its fine to get confused every once in a while young one the world and all that happens within it makes for complicated existence." He smiles and stretches yawning lightly " was there anything else you wished to discuss young idrialla"

Idri fidgeted in her chair she knew from his tone and question it was time to go. " nos.."

"come then i shall take you back to Easur i am sure your mom or guard perhaps both " he said with a grin.." are looking for you"

Idri looked a bit guilty but nodded. " yes's is likely..mes gonna be grounded for awhile"

Vaul chuckled and took her back to Dragonborn Keep on Easur where a worried Deaden and Wolfen were indeed searching for her.

....

She laughed as she trapped the demon with in a prison in away of his own making as he had come after her and her crew true they had stolen the mask from the demon, and he had beaten most of them up quite soundly killing at least 6 of them.

Had he not done what he had he would have won the fight killing them all. Faeril looked extreamly battered and was on the verge of passing out from blood loss, her vision spotty at best.

The demon had sent a tornado of flame at her but had been walking inside of it along the beach where she and the crew had been hidng out. The mask she had stolen was payment she owed a friend of hers.

Seeing he was inside of the tornado of flame and all the sand that was being swept up inside of it melting as he moved she used what energy she had left to cool the flames as to freeze it and make the elements involved fuse together to create a solid tornado looking prison of glass around the demon..

Lachlen had escaped with the mask as ordered.

She could hear it now cursing them from inside the prison.. it wouldnt take long with its strength to free itself.. but it would bide them time.

She just hoped her friend knew what she was getting herself into and could handle it, but now she considered her debt paid in full.

She did not know who lifted her in there arms and carried her away she collapsed and did not wake again for a week.

Durring that time while she slept immages begain filling her mind she tossed and turned in her sleep faces she did not recognize aside from vukans begain surficing, battles, conversations laughing training and so much more, however she could not hold onto them and veaguly remembered any of it when she did awaken.

“she sure has the devils own luck, last few fights she shouldnt have survived..”

“aye but what she comes away with an what we earn be worth it.. even the loss of some of the men.”

“True.. what if she ever finds..” there was sudden silence as a hand covered someones mouth” shuhhh you fool. not another word” the voices faded off and Faeril didnt know if she dreamed them or if it had been real.

“What about the little fellow who brought her to us what do we do with him?” Lachlen smiled shaking his head. “ That be for the captin to decide once she wakes. Ariana came to speak with the captin now were safe from the demon.”

“so long as she dont stay long i dont want another run in wi tha one.”

Faeril woke, and called for food as well as drink to be brought, she dressed while she waited and told Lachlen sr. to let Ariana in.

As soon as Arina entered Faeril spoke. She was partially dressed she had her leggings and boots on as well as her white blouse but not her corset or jacket as of yet..

she stood slowly so as not to appear too weak facing Ariana.

“Consider tha yer payment fer helpin me out o a bit o a spot lass..i’ll drop ye a the next port .. we be headed fer pompe. I turst tha will be satisfactory enough.. The demon we stole tha from will be huntin fer it, an nerly go us.. ye ken tha right?”

when Arina grinned and nodded Faeril shrugged and said “ sa be it ye ken fen fer yerself well enough.. hower if ye needs me in future..” Ariana saluted her and left the cabin.

The ship rocked to and fro on the waves. The sea was calm for the time bing but such could easly change. Faeril sat on the edge of her desk for a moment looking out the window of her cabin quite pleased with herself, and her crew. Tho Lachlen was starting to get on her nerves.

He entered with the food she had ordered and a bottle of rum, " Bring me the one who returned me ta the ship i would meet this one. " Lachelen sr. left the cabin to find the little male called shamus.

....

Weeks later fully recovered Faeril's eyes were hidden by the shadows cast this night her shape and that of her men bairly seen in the thick heavy fog as they made there way down the streets and allys ways of the town. Her men had there orders and begain carring them out as cannon fire roared in the distance a wicked half grin touched her lips.

Argos stopped in his tracks he and sevral others had begun heading for the docs at the sound of cannon fire the bells of the town ringing out as cyrs of pirates attacking begain spreading like wilde fire.

He grabed his friend Grey Valentine's arm stopping him pointing down another ally. " what is it" Valentine asked. Grey owed Argos his life and would remain his loyal friend until his last breath. Argo's eyes met his friends breifly his brow furrowed thoughtfully " im not sure something dosent sit right i thought i scented... Wyn but.. she wouldnt"

Argos shook his head saying mearly " come " before taking off in the oposite direction of the docs Valentine following closely at his side the two never far from one another, he never understood why his friend didnt assoceate much with his fellow damarians visiting his neice Ade and great niece only on rare occasions.

Argos he knew had loved his sister Idrialla greatly and both he and Valentine had dedicated there lives to her memorie. What she had represented and stood for. Helping to bring freedom to others not only on the earthly realm but in others too.

Valentine paused when his friend stopped and looked around the area for anything out of place as Argos spoke " this is wrong.. it is Wynwillow im scenting, move back she and others are approching"

The two moved back around a corner crouching down behind some crates they were in luck as they were down wind. They watched as the pirates approched the few she had with her " Argos Wyn looks like that female pirate weve been hearing about of late." Argos waved a hand to silence him Valentine grew quiet as they watched.

Argos cursed under his breath, she cant mean to go after.. how did she even know .. Argos stepped out of the fog into the lantern light " Thats far enough DruidOak.. care to tell me what your game is ?"

Valentine remained in the shadows the fog aiding him but took careful aim covering argos with the single shot pistol he had.

Faeril turned to look at him there was no recognition of him upon her features which troubled Argos a bit there should have been some tell tell sign a flare of nostrals, a widening of the eyes a tilt of the head but there was nothing.

He could see a scar at her temple that hadnt been there before her pink tented eyes gleamed in the lantern light as she focused on him she was dressed not in her ushual pirate garb but actully in the damarian armor she had worn when they had retaken Easur. Argos didnt know what was going on. It was Wyn and yet not.

"im afraid lad, handsome tho ye be, i've no time ta answer yer questions. Ye ken tell yer frien ta come out as well .. as ta me games" she grinned and Argo's eyes widened it took all he had not to step back as she countinued speaking " yell ha ta play alon ta find out"

With tht she changed from her human form to her true damarian form and flew up into the tower of the building. Argos having lunged for her in an attempt to grab her was shocked for he had missed having grabbed nothing but air.

Ether he wa getting rusty or wyn had vastly improved her skilles sense he had encountered her last. Valentine had stepped out into the lamp light next to him looking up into the night where the female had gone. " a keen woman that one, and dangerous, I can try a binding spell if we can get close to her"

argos looked over at him appearing a bit frustrated as he shook his head " no not yet beisdes i dont think its wyn were dealing with .. not entierly she didnt seem to now me .. we need more answers"

"Have you considered a look a like ? " At that question Argos grinned and shook his head " ohh no.. you dont know Wyn but if you truly knew her you'd know there isnt another like her anywhere"

Before Grey could agree or disagree more shouts of alarm and mayhem broke loose as prisoners ere rleased from the prisons Argos cursed " you help the humans valentine i'll go after her and see what i can discover" Grey or rather Valentine didnt like the idea of leaving his friend but did as instructed wondering himself what indeed was going on.

In human form Argo's was 6ft 2in' in hight build around 220lbs athletic and lean his blonde hair beginning to turn silver as his sister's years before had done, was dressed much as a lord and peer of the realm might be a sherrif or magestrate might be.. Taking up such positions allowed for the freedom he needed to help others albet not as swiftly as he might like at times.

Upon entering the building he took on a form more familiar and comfortable to him that of a lion man he could have taken on his true damarian form but hed never been comfortable or happy in his true skin so to speak and so had adpoted this one.

Faeril smerked as Argos joined hr tossing a rather large saphire between her hands back and forth having been expecting one or both of the two she had met below she threw it to him as he entered. Argos caught it out of reflex and glared at her " Whats all this about Wyn ?, is someone in trouble are you being forced to steel this isnt your normal occupation?"

She laughed a full bodied laugh as he watched she wiped a tear from her eye from having been laughing and sobered looking much more serious as she spoke " I am no this Wyn ye seem ta be confusin me wi .. allow me ta introduce meself.. i be Faeril.. an i be a pirate.. this.. be wha i do.."

Argos paled, or would have looked pale had he been in human form rather than his lion like one. None had actually seen Faeril before but the roomers that were growing and spreading far and wide.. hadnt been given much credit a female captin.

Tho he had known wyn and others .. many thoughts were flying through Argos mind most of them random.. how had Wyn become Faeril .. still more questions no answere's he needed to hold her and contact the other Damarians.

As if she were reading his mind she said " if yer thinkin ta catch me lad ye best ha some interestin skill an move fast fer im afraid yer time an mine be up " Before he had time to react he just suddenly couldnt breath he was robbed of air.. slowly as he sunk to his knees and the world took on a fuzzy over look fading to black all he heard was.

"Dunna worrie ill no kill ye jus rest " Argos was furious when Valentine woke him later and she was gone along ith all the gems and coin that had been in the tower save for one peace the large saphire she had tossed to him.

Valentine simply remained silent for a time before finelly speaking up " Sir unles you intend to persue her yourself you must conctact " he shut up as Argos shot him a look sighing he knew Argos didnt like having to deal with any of the others.

They reminded him too muc hof his sister's and parent's loss, but if they were to continue in the positions they gained here they would needs concact others who could persue her, or give up there pretense of being human.

Valentine watched as Argos straightned away from the window where he had paused in his pacing Argos nodded to him stepping into the other room as he took human form and motioned for his friend to watch the door as he pulled a small crystal from the pouch at his belt and used it to contact Easur.

it was Rhannon who answered him, and filled him in on what little she knew of Wynwillows disaperance and he her on what Wyn, or rather Faeril had said.

"Dont worrie about Wyn or Faeril.. i already have others out who have been looking for Wyn i will up date them, and send them after her. dont change your plans in what your doing. Tell the humans youve hired others to hunt down thos responcable and do what you can there"

Argos didnt like it he actually wanted to hunt her down himself, but Rhannon and even he knew Grey when he put his two cents in would have a point and they couldnt blow what they had already been working on.

....

While on board ship already well on there way out to the further reaches of the sea.

"Yer playin a dangerous game capin" Faeril leaned back in her chair kicking her feet up onto the corner of her desk. Inside the capbin of her ship. she interlaced her fingers behind her head. The serious look in her eyes belying the humerous quark to her lips letting Lachlen know she was in a good mood but he'd best watch his tone.

"i am well aware o what tis i be doin.. are ye questionin me Lachlen ? " He shifted uncomfortably under her direct gaze " Nay im not .. just wonderin where yer headed wi all this the men be pleased wi the boody an all bu we be drawn a lot o atteniton"

He backed up as her feet touched the floor but before he could turn to even attempt to get out the door he was slamed up against it, her arm up against his throat. Gods she was fast he hadnt even seen her move other than when hed seen her sit up.

He couldnt talk he could bairly breath. All he could do was keep still and listen, his head hurt as well from having hit the door she glared up at him and then pulling him away from the wall threw him with ease across the cabin.

He crashed into her desk which was bolted to the floor and lay where he landed not fool enough to rise right away. He waited as she walked around placing her booted foot upon his chest bending her knee resting one hand on it as she looked down at his pathetic form she smiled. " ye oer step yerself seems ye need reminden o who is in charge here"

He swallowed waiting as she rolled her eyes, and steped back from him " Ge up ye piftiful excuse.. me plans are me own.. i tell ye what ye need ta ken when tis time.. did ye er wonder why en tho ye rescued me i still ha na taken ye inta me confidence ?"

Slowly he got ot his feet angry but not daring to say a word well aware he had pushed her enough or as much as he dared he nodded to her waiting to hear what it was she had to say.

Faeril crossed her arms over her chest her eyes gleaming " i dunna trust ye. Aye ye tol me me name .. ye tol me we were in a battle an ye saved me life.. bu ye will na tell me mun else.. an i fin it hard ta beleive ye dunna ken anythin else when ye remember all else.. now Ge out o me cabin afore i really lose me temper.."

She moved so that he could get by her and watched him leave the cabin shaking her head, once he was gone she began to relax some and cleaning up the mess she had made by tossing Lochlen around but the fool was geting to the point where she might just kill him.

She knew she was drawing attention and wanted to attacking the ports for additional booty tested her skilles as well as her mens they were under orders to kill only the men who engaged them in combat no women or children else they faced her.

Merchent ships were becoming to boring a target but still profitable for the crew, other pirates would ocme out after them thinking to ether stop her antics or steel what she and her crew had gained. Ether way antoher test of skills and advancement of hers and the crews reputation..

Going up on deck she directed her helmsmen to set corse for Pompeii time to sail different waters for a time. She returned below her thoughts turning to there latest venture and the one in the tower.

The male in the tower seemed familar to her tho how or why she didnt know she walked over to the cabinet in her cabin, and pulled out a decanter for rum.

Chapter 12

She needed to get going there was an item she had heard of she wanted to get hold of and see if the lil devil of a lepercan were tellin the truth o it if she er got her hands on him again she would find a way to kill the bugger.....

The Lech had robbed them blind after helping them amass a fortune, saying he was taking it in payment of a coat she owed him then vanished. She'd nearly had a mutiny on her hands and had taken care o that right enough.. now they had to find a specific place on this blasted earth to open the rift to the realm they needed.

in a pouch at her waist she also carried with her the crystals she sought so that should she encounter Jeral again she would be ready..

What she wasnt aware of was that her first mate had over heard her telling the other crewmen to meet with Vukan, and bring him aboard if he showed. Lachlen then made his own plans.

Telling the other after Faeril had left that if he wished to live he would do as Lachlen told him and lead Vukan to a slavers ship instead that specilized in demon kind the origonal crafts men of the magical chains that held demons, Dragons and more powerless.

Lachlen made arangements with the slavers and as soon as Vukan was lead aboard and looking for Wyn.. Faeril. He was hit from behind and knocked unconsious then chained.. he hadnt had a chance to use his abilitys taken unawares Lachlen grinned and paid the slavers then returned to Faerils ship.. with her none the wiser.

He knew if she ever discoverd his betrayel not only his lying to her about who she truly was and what she was, but what he had done to Vukan he was a dead man but so long as her memoire was lost and she continued to take the poweders..

He cursed Vukan having told her not to take any more. She had listened to him and so he had to sneek it in a few of her drinks and thanked the gods there was no taste and no oder else he would not be able to continue.. still he had to be cautious.

he didnt understand why she didnt turn to him as she aught to have.. after all he had saved her life.. the only thing wrong with this plan however was that Ferial altho Vukan handnt joined them took his advice and no longer took the poweders Lachlen would give..

....

The Winking Shepherd Tavern's sign swayed in the wind. The lanterns light in the windows and candles glow from the verious tables called weary travelers like a beccon in the night to pause and rest or drink before moving on there way light conversation could be heard garbled sounds really noting dicernable over what music if one could call it that played.

The womans eyebrows raise. " hmmm... not exactly what i'd call power. it is a gift though."

She gave a small nod. "I can understand your situation. The snow takes quite a while to get used to." She takes another sip out of her tankard. Feeling the liquid burn and tingle down her throat and to her stomach.

She gave a satisfied shiver at the feeling. “Im Ryllea by the way.” she murmered.

“Without his gift we could not breath and Her fires would die to ash. That gift alone is worth love and worship.” He’d smirk “But if you ask for powers of Lor’Shal he gave to us Argrosh, a metal that weaves the air around it. With skill of a smith and blessing of a priest this metal can have many different uses.”

....

Faeril had heard of this tavern in her travels and decided to pay it a visit to discover what she may this was only part of the many conversations she heard going on before stepping threw its doors.

....

A male in tavern would smirk as the woman spoke and gave her name. He nods in greeting and looks into her eyes “I am Darien though most call me Dar.” it was an uncommon name for an Elvish man but he was named from a human female, which was a rather long story of his past but he usually never found the need to explain nor did many ask him about it.

“Well it is nice to meet you Dar. So what brought you to this place?” She smiled as she leaned forward in her seat, drumming her long fingers on the wooden table.

Darien’s eyes widened a bit as she leaned forward her dress making her bossoms and cleveage noteable. He turns his head slightly as to try and not stare, though he did get a good look. He smirks “Well the same as you I assume, simply traveling an urge to see foreign lands.”

....

Faeril opened the tavern door and stepped inside she serveyed the interrior before making her way over to an empty table she sat down

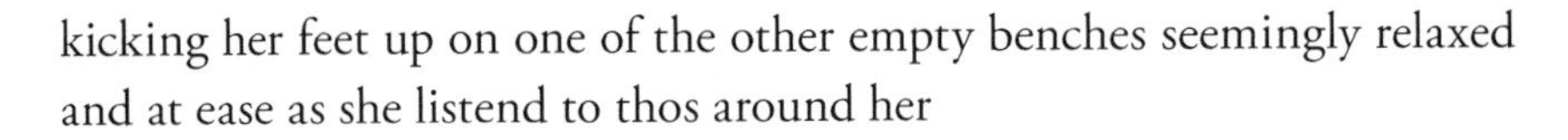

kicking her feet up on one of the other empty benches seemingly relaxed and at ease as she listend to thos around her

---

“We elves often love to travel, dont we? We live far too long to be able to stay in one place for too long” She murmers as she runs her fingers through her hair, slowly weaving and unweaving her hair while she speaks.

another female enters the cavern shivering, covered in snow

He nods and chuckles a bit at her comment. An Elf always spoke so commonly of how they stayed youthful in appearance and aged to live well beyong many others but they never usually spoke on their actual age. “Indeed so very true. That incling of an itch when we sit still for far to long.”

The woman would walk to Dar and smile at him “ I noticed your toungue, would you like to see a trick of mine?”

The fiend would yawn slowly the calm of night soothing to him as he lifts the tankard of mead to his lips one more sipping from it the pungent sweetness tantalizing upon his pallet

He cocked a brow at the woman his orange slitted eyes gleaming as a smirk tugged at the edge of his mouth. “Go ahead my dear, I am interested.”

The woman would grin as the air around her shimmered laughing as she took another swig of her drink. “Aye. I must say that is true. I have seen many lands, of varying temperatures and climates. Each one had its own unique appeal.”

He nodded once more “That they have, and I am quite pleased with the treasure I have found here.” He was referring to her beauty and could not take his eyes from hers. “Though rare gems are hard to come by.”

Faerils gaze would wonder over thos present assessingly taking note of there wepons even as she listend to them. she had yet to speak after entering the banter back and forth the music here was lively and touched apart o her soul she found she enjoyed it quite a lot.

one kept drawing her gaze tho she knew him not his scent was some how familiar he was grey skinned with red eyes black of hair with long black horns that curved back a fleeting memorie stired with in her.

The pain such immages brought soon pushed it out and she hid it well anoyed at this she shook her head and looked for a tavern maid to ask for a draft of rum to be brought laying a coin down to pay.

....

“Treasure?” she questioned. A small eyebrow quirking upwards toward her hairline. “I used to posses many fine gems and jewels, but I left them behind many years ago. All but this,” she motioned to the small stone hanging around her neck.

His eyes widened as his mouth gaped slightly. Quickly he without a care fell to the floor on his knee, his eyes never leaving her. “By Her love...I did not fathum your form...” His pupils darked back and forth over her form, his eyes drinking in what he saw.

....

The woman would stand up and slither over to the woman who looked as if she needed a drink I can serve you my dear, what would you like?

Faeril would nod and smile “ Thank ye Rum.. if ye ha it”

He chuckled and found that she mistook his gesture cute. “Indeed a rare gem around your neck only to compliment the beautiful woman wearing it.” he could not have been more forward or blunt with his words this time.

Faerils ears turned this way and that as she caught the words treasure.. then grinned reolizing he ment the lass -

"I have nearly any drink you could desire and a few more things besides " she would enter the kitchen coming out a short time later with the woman's rum

"Thank ye lass " Faeril slides the coin across the table to her.

....

A red blush creeped up her neck, across her cheeks and nearly reached her forehead. "Oh.....my...."She tapped her fingers on the table and giggled. "Thank you Dar. That was quite kind of you." Her lashes fluttered softly, shyly kissing her tanned cheeks as she glanced over at him.

The fiend Lichen would drain down the last drops of the pungent mead licking his pale grey lips lightly before a soft yawn would slip out the thought of rest ever so appealing after his travels of late.

He nods and smiles and then looks to the owner and sees she is busy not wanting to bother her for a drink at the moment she seemed rather occupied. "Of course it is so easy to compliment one such as yourself when all one must do is speak simple truths."

"Your form is wonderous, you can will your appearance to change?" He stood back up looking at her before looking about for his stool, after pulling it back he'd sit again leaning towards her in wonderment. His people's magic was control of elements but nothing of such magnitude.

"Yes my dear, to nearly any creature I can think of"

With a small chuckle and a shake of her head she lifted her gaze to meet her eyes. Emerald meeting silver-green. "I am almost worried that these are lines you often use to bed a woman you meet in a tavern. They seem to....."She pondered a momen, tapping a finger on her chin "Well rehearsed" "and several forms of human"

....

Faeril would rise taking her rum with her to join the being who seemed to be drawing her gaze. he seemed the most challange in the room at present however looks she knew were deceving as she drew closer she caught a glimps of an immage flashing of a battle fought with one who looked similar to this one.

she leaned against the wall a frown upon her features as the immage cleard she crossed her ankles for all the world appearing to have leaned against it apuropouse and downed half the rum in her cup before straitining and stepping twords him once again.. " care fer a wee bit o company ?"

....

He chuckles a bit wildly finding her comment ammusing. he was a silver tongue one good with words and speaking of poetry. "I assure you I nay rehearse what I say." he continues to chuckle enjoying it all to much. He looks about and calls out raising a hand to grab ones attention. "I need another drink for the lady here and one of the same for me."

"That truely is amazing, I have never seen such a thing since I have left my homeland." He smirked to her as his fist rested on his jaw line still he looked her over.

she would smile at Kane "A gift of my birth"

the Young Valkyrian Warrior entered the tavern with curiousity and much need of a drink. She stood tall still in uniform. Her deep blue eyes servaying the Tavern with Caution and Intruige

she would stand up and Slither to the woman who had entered the Tavern and smile at her" Hello and welcome to the Four Nymphs, how may I serve you"

She gave a small smile. “A bit of Ale maybe please? May I sit?” She asked politely.

Kane’s gaze followed Silver as she moved away. His tongue slithered from his mouth again to taste the magic left hanging in the air from her transformation. The long tongue coiled and hooked once before slurping back behind his lips.

Shortly after his call a woman with drinks in hand saunters over a bit seductively and smiles with a giggle placing them down before glarring him over. He shakes his head a bit before giving the woman coin and she sauntered back off.

“Please seat yourself anywhere and I’ll be right back with your ale “she would raise her voice to be heard “ Does anyone else need anything? Besides me of course “she would giggle

....

Lichen would look up at the woman his eyes appraising the being for any threat she she might be as was necceasary for one of his background. “Im not one for whom comapny is plentiful if you wish to sit beside me as I drink and consider what mortals see in thier life upon midgard then I shall not deny you such”

....

Lichen would call out “a frosted ale is you please, and yes you may join me”

Ryllea smiled and pushed her empty tankard away before taking the second. She chewed gently on her lower lip, reddening it further before lifting the tankard to her lips and taking a sip. “Well, I suppose knowing you arent rehearsed is flattering”

she chuckled a bit and raised her cup to him taking a seat finding herself liking this fellow wether she discovered anything of use or not this eve she did find the tavern itself rather to her liking and so would caus no trouble with in it unless an oprotuninty presented itself.

"Warmed bourbon if you could, Mistress Silver." He called over his shoulder to her.

"Ok thats Ale, Frosted Ale and Warmed Bourbon...anything else "she would smile sweetly

he nods to Ry as she took the tankard and he would lift his ever so slightly "To good company, and a beautiful veiw." he states before lifting the rim of the tankard to his lips the froth adorn the top of the contents tickling his upper lip as he tilts it upward taking a rather large swig.

Lichen would continue to observe the woman out of the corner of his eye he had wandered all fo the worlds one could reach through the use of great bridge Bifrost and had not seen a world where he might guess a being of her particuler kind would be from

"So what brings one dressed for the sea and with a sailors tounge to this place with snow thickly blanketing the ground and forests around us?"

The fiend would smile and accept the ale sipping from it and enjoying the cold sensation it left upon his lips and down his thrat asd he partook of it a soothing sensation he was quite accustom to.

....

You are most welcome." His eyes still to hers starring deeply as if drawn into the sespools that led to ones very being or soul. He smiles into the tankard taking another large swig from the contents a bit slipping from the corners of his mouth which was quickly corrected as he wiped it on the sleeve of his tunic.

Katerina held her Ale close to her. "Thank you Ma'am." Her eyes at the glass infront of her.

She smiled at him as he drank. "So Dar, tell me about yourself"

....

Faeril chuckled as she sat next to him continuing to listen to all going on around them as he drank down the ale he had requested

"Lichen I would have put your drink between my breasts but it was too darn cold, next time order something warmer" The server stated to the fiend as Faeril took her seat smerking at the banter between them.

"Held fast by a lovely bossom and warmed by beauty, could it be any warmer?" He smirked to her as his right arm rose from the table's edge, his gloved fingertips pressed at the tankard's rim before gripping it firm to lift it from her. "Such a caring creature you are my dear." He'd nod to her as his smirk grew before sipping from his drink.

He smirked placing the tankard down and nods to her "But of course." He clears his throat and stands climbing up onto the table as he was always one for a good show, or rather being a tad dramatic.

"Picture this...." He exclaimed loudly "The sun rising just over the horizon reaching its tendrils out upon the fields chasing the remaining shadows of the night away. The breeze od spring blowing year round, breaking through the groaning trees as their limbs rattle singing aloud rejoicing.

The great lands of Morian, far to the South of here where the trees stand taller then any mans castle and are great for climbing. Where wild beasts roam free, and the Elflings play of music and singing as they dance in the forest.

A land so majestical that we dare not cut from them, or build but rather live within what was so graciously provided for us." he was enthusiastic when it came to his home land and it was apparent."

The fiend would look at silver and grin "it does not suit my tounge to partake in hot drinks miss silver but I am sure many a mortal man would jump at the chance to recieve a warm 'brew' from that particuler treasure 'chest" He smirks and again partakes in the chilled ale

she would look at the man causing a scene in her tavern* Perhaps you were right Fiend, we should have let that one languish a bit longer.

Ryllea laughed and shook her head. "Why are you on the table? I thought it was just you and I talking? Must you bring in te whole tavern?" She almost snapped, but caught herself at the last moment.

....

Faeril still grinning would down the rest of her rum setting the cup down then look over at him "ahh lad do ye figure out what i am yell ha ta le me know fer i dunna ken it meself .. took a wound ta the head ye see.. me old crew from wha me first mate tells me died in the explosion tha ga me this.. as fer me presents here.. well now i heard o this place an im always game fer a good drught o rum er two"

She signaled to the waitress for another round setting another coin on the table, finnishing off what was in her first before setting the tankered down to finnish answering his question.

"well there be another reason i be in lan bu tha buisness be me own " Faeril's pink colored eyes danced with mischeif " an aye the sea as well as the skys no matter the ship the feel o her decks beneath me feet as she moves be mur home ta me then any harth thus far .. tell me a bit o yer self ye reminde me o someone tho i canna place him in me mind"

"I am not but one who grew tired of the gales of my home and decided to I was unlike my kin whom were contented to live like beasts in niflheim save for those like my self whom have fed upon the essance of an entity that embodies pride. My 'brother' as it were like my self traverse the words in search for a purpose for our gifts my purpose is one I keep to my self"

The feind replyed finding himself curious about this being and enjoying gaging her in converstation. "What would you like to know my dear?" The fiend asked of the being next to him

Faeril continued speaking with the fiend as the others continued there own privet conversations where all could hear "we are similar in tha a least then would ye care fer another round o what er yer drinkin..? on me o corse"

the grin having never truly left her lips her foot tapped in rythem to the music keeping the beat easly as if it came naturlly to her " ye say yer brother travels the realms as well as ye.. may haps tis he who ye remind me o"

"The fiend looked thoughtful and nodded "very possible there is an entire brood of other fiends who learned to traverse the worlds and if you are a traveler there would be a chance you might have encountered one of them, and no I dont require any more ale what I have is sufficiant to keep my throat cool and dry"

"ohh aye " Faeril laughs softly " i travel i ha no home sa i make me own where er i be.. " Her head came up alertly and she tilted her head to the side her ears moivng this way and that as if listining to something.

Rising looking back at him again she bowed as if she had done it a thousand times in a most courtly mannor her eyes never turly leaving his however as she straitened she said " i must take me leave o ye hower i shall return another eve.. tho no in th near future i be thinkin if all goes well twas a plesure ta meet ye i be called Faeril .."

"I shall remember the name miss Faeril and you may call me Lichen"

"Lichen.. i'll no fer get ye lad.. " she turned and left the tavern definatly planning to return again another evening.

Chapter 13

Finnaly her men had discovered where she would be able to open the rift to take them threw to where they need be to gain the object she sought.. she joined them on deck taking over the healm she charted there corse and powered the crystals to the freqancy needed a devilish glint in her eyes as she guided the ship threw..-

Faeril left her men save her first mate on ship after it emerged in the realm they had been seeking she gave orders for them to keep the ship at ready for a fast escape should it be necessary her eyes flashed excitedly it wasnt so much the objects that drew her as it was the danger involved and the thrill of sucess.

The goods she devided among the crew keeping none herself tho this object she may she would decide that later she glided down her first mate at her side a demon but of a different type his hands and back badly burned but they hidndered him not.

carefully and slowly they begain searching the realm for the object they sought until they came at last to the area Vaul resided in Faeril often stopping her second in command from taking this or that reminding him they were after one object and one alone on this voyage.. she motioned him to take one direction around the chamber they entered as she took the other.

Vaul had chosen to reside within the land he could only call home where the wind and mist galed endlessly with a cold deeper than any that most would know living upon earth and whisps of shadows and black ice scattered amongst the world.

The perfect home for the malevolent beings that resided here and from it all Vaul had sought piece in what oter would call abyss and such peace was his until he felt the pressence of others.

His eyes opened wide his senses spanning far beyond the scope of the mundane a weiry and tired expression as if the thought of being awake was more than he could bear he would call out "If you value the breath in thy lungs then flee if not then stay and die"

The building would shake violently a thick unyielding pressence filling it as the cieling walls and and the very floor should slowly shift and shpe itself into minions to Vauls will imps, demons, and all other manner of creatures the fiend had known in his trevsl would form restlessly aiming to clense the fiends home of intruders.

Faeril cursed whoever lived here had discovered them but she would not be detured she took up a defensive stance her eyes glittering with dangerous intent as the walls shook and the voice sounded a slight curve not quite a grin but close touched her lips.

she drew her sword turning it over again in her hand as the imps and minnor demons emerged from out of the floor ceiling and other crevices she used her ability with air to push them out of her way only killing when it was necessary to escape there grasps.

her first mate however had no such objectoins and killed as many as he could calling " Captin we must go.. there be too many youll not find it now."

Faeril didnt hear him as she had rounded a corner and ducked into another room the object she saught if the discription she had been given matched was there among other treasures however she wasnt interested in the others not at present.

Vaul could sense the taking of an object he valued highly the heart of a demon whose power had long kept any denezin of this realm from wandering into his halls "very well... I suppose I shall have to deal with this my self"

Vaul would rise from his throne like seat the building again rumbling as the stone given life would freeze in its tracks it power drawn once more into Vaul as he walked with a solmn tread through the halls his pressence a stiffling thickness in the air walking towards where he felt the intruder and ruby heart both

Faeril felt the thickining of the air and knew something or someone was coming that would be something worth facing and reckoning with she stepped back masking her scent by building a berrier of sworling air.

That barrier kept her scent down wind and away from the entrances she slipt the gem into a pouch and looped its strings threw her belt loop tieing them off securly a slight grin touching her lips as she drew her sword prepairing for who or what would come.

The fiend Vaul would burst into the room never moving his face from his intended target hs extended senses keeping him well appraised on the actions of the woman.

As he drew near her one hand making a mock jab in her direction. The chain hanging from his hip extending in connection with his jabbing punch the weighted hamer striking towards her with intense physical force-

Faeril very nearly took the blow a split seconds shock at seeing one of the beings who she recognized in her dreams tho she rememberd not his name who looked so like the fiend she had left behind in a tavern another realm had held her in place.

she turned her head just seconds before he would have connected stepping to the side at the same instance the sworling berrier of air would also help to throw off his aim but not by much.

Given he had walked into it with out much issue he was to close to bring her sword around and from a slashing angle however that didnt stop her from using other means as his fist went past her she would bring her knee up into his stomach intending to double him over if sucessful would then bring her sword hilt down on his head or upper sholders to knock him over.

Vauled would take the knee striking into his stomach but his reaction time would be impecable the chain striking the wall behind her shattering the wall and the momentum pushing him back out of her reach as the other chain opposite of the first one would grinds against the cieling.

stirking downward in an attempt to hit her shoulder then coil around her as he slips just out of the range of her sword, ominous red eyes locking onto her and a short instance of confusion would overwhelm him as her identity would register. "... w..wyn? is that you..."

As the wall shattered behind her and he was pushed back out of reach seeing the second one shoot up wards and hiting the celing she dived and summersaluted across the groud coming up on her feet drawing a dagger throwing it at him with a very accurate and deadly aim.

as the chain came back down to to indeed strike her sholder she didnt quite get to her feet but did manage to bring her sword up to slice the chain in two damarian enchanted steel tho she didnt know it.

To her it was simply her sword she stood to face him she heard him speak and saw some confusion on his features.." i be Faeril tho i dunna ken exactly who ye be, er when we met..afor no that is.."

The long sleep had effected the fiends mind he wished to escape reality here in Niflheim and so his thoughts were cloudy still facts not crisp or clear as they often did. "wha...what is a damarians doing in the lands of pride? why are you here distrubing me when I all i want is to be left alone!" His aura around him would become pungant shattering the ground beneath his feet as he shouted-

"A what ?? " she asked clearly confused Vukan had called her a Damarian as well however she didnt stay that way long a bit of her own pride flashin in her eyes as she answered part of his question " I dunna Ken wha a Damarian is lad but i ha what i came fer an ill be a goin if ye be so kind ill leave ye ta yer rest"

with a nod and a grin as well she made to stride right past him and out the door way as if he would simply let her pass she knew he wouldnt but if she could confuse him enough perhaps she wouldnt have to hurt him too badly. she liked the other she had met at the tavern and didnt really want to hurt his kin and something told her she knew this one as well and didnt want to hurt him ether.

The ground before faeril would burst like a piller extending from the ground to strike her back into the waiting embrace of Vauls first chain which with one sweeping motion would coil around her continuing its swinging motion to slam her into the floor.

Then wall the fiends mind no longer in its usual state and merly concerned with defending that which belonged to the fiend "You shall take nothing of mine it is all needed to keep those I wish to not be bothered by from entering this place"

Vaul would toss Faeril across the room from his chain then rush towards her his left arm glowing with his thick red aura punching as he nears the point of landing a shockwave of his aura lightly striking that entire side of the room

Faerils pink colored eyes glittered dangerously as the puller burst from the floor sending her flying she did a back flip in the air righting herself but wasnt quite fast enough to avoid the waiting chain that wrapped around her and slamed her into the ground/

she was winded for a moment as he spoke she regained her breath saying " i'm no done yet lad dunna think me sa easly defeated " manipulating the air currents gathering the energy letting it build holding onto it as he threw her she spun like a top in the air.

Opening her wings catching herself hovering above the ground as he came at her she hit him with a fist of air pressure gathered together releasing it so that it would strike with in feet of her still this was not the worst she could do if she wished however again she was reluctent to use such tactics.

The blast of her air pressure fist would strike him unprepared sending him flying but his reaction was swift landing on his feet his hands outstreched blasting a concussive burst of his aura aimed at his flying foe.

There his chain gripping one of the rocks of rubble upon the floor the size of a human head and tossing it right after his cunccusive blast of aura so the ripple in the air would hide its coming strike aimed at her mid section

As the blast of aura much like that of a sound wave rippeld threw the air she closed her eyes feeling the change in the currents of air and built up a rippling wave to counter it however that didnt stop the already forward momentum of the rock behind it.

It did indeed connect and knock her from the air into the far wall cracking a rib or two in the process she slid down the wall pushing the rock away from her as much as she was able and unsteadly got to her feet " damn me yer bloody good .. who are ye ? damn ye.."

He would Pivot forward the damage of the air pressure fist now more apprant as a trickle of blood would slip out of his mouth and a burst of his aura senidng him towards her in attack to react while she is unable to defends herself.

His left hand clasping onto her neck "surrender back what you have stolen and leave or I will squeeze the life from you" His eyes would remain glazed over from his altered state of mind

Her own eyes flashed not with fear but with anger and pride she would gather the air around them and then begin drawing the air from his lungs starving him and cutting off his air.

Even as he choaked her they would see who passed out first thinking only take it if you can.. not wishing to waist preshous seconds or air she allowed her body to relax and concentrated on robbing him of air

He would gag at the constriction of his aura his grip upon her throat tightening as he would let aura flow into his free hand striking it into her chest with the last of his strength as he would feel his conciousness slip.

she would black out as he hit her stomach knocking what reamined of her air from her as soon as she lost consiousness his air flow would return to normal she would go lax in his hands and as she slipped into that unconsiousness.

No longer fighting her mind picked up his scent as well as his sight and took her back to pervious encounters not as Faeril but as Wyn.. leading to other memories of Vukan, Adewen and so much more.... her pulse did he choose to let her live would be weak bairly dicernable, but there.

Vaul would fall to his knees breathing deeply and letting go of the woman to let her unconcious body fall onto the floor Vauls own hands at his neck attempting to catch his breath a burning sensation in his throat.

His mind would slowly become more clear and in horror he would look at Wynwillow laying there, and would reach twords her with a worried expression fearing he had slain her. Lightly resting to fingers onto her neck to feel her pulse.

He breathed a deep sigh of relief “Thank pride shes still alive” He would weakly pick up wyn craddling her with his arms. Striding on shaky legs to a room of his realm and setting her down onto a bed he had never used.

Walking to the corner still catching his breath distressed he had been in so little control of his actions "you should feel lucky lady wyn... death or worse is what you could have expected had you lost to most fiends"

Faerils first mate watched from a distance as his captin was carried off to another room clearly having lost the battle and cursed he recognized Vaul even if Vaul didnt recognize him Lachlen was a shape shifter that had helped in reclaiming Easur.

One of few idri had only just begun training before her death, but had not wanted to remain on Easur so had joined Wyns crew and been apart of it until the exploson he had to get the ship and crew out of here before she woke.

If anyone could get her to remember who she was it was him he had gotten rid of Vukan by sending him on board the wrong ship and selling him to demon slavers. If she rememberd, and started asking questions.

He shook his head and flead tho he had saved her life he had lied to her after and even if she forgave that what he did to Vukan wouldnt be forgiven. he was a dead man on borrowed time.

Vaul would summon a stone thrall minion to grip the blood ruby made from a demons heart to return it to its proper place the fiend himself leaning against the corner of the room waiting for Wyn to awaken so he could decide what next to do.

Wynwillow woke her head hurting like hell along with her throat and the rest of her body she groned softly. Slowly she tryed to sit up a bit disorented trying to figure out where she was as her surroundings were unfamillar. she wasnt able to sit up long winced in pain as she lay back down closing her eyes " bloody hell.. " she grumbled " each breath hurt it was a familiar sinsation she had apprently brused or broken ribs again.

The question was how had she gotten here. The last thing she remembered was getting ready to face her father in battle.

Vaul spoke his voice partialy fileld with subtle humor and partial coughs "my apollgoes for the aches and pains miss Wyn but if you had been hoping to surprise me a simple message would have sufficed rather then breaking in while your alternate identity picks a fight and starts nicking all the little trasure she can grab, but if its any consolation you did get some good hits while we both were not our selves"

"Vaul ??.. " she tryed to move to look at him and groned " ohh" that was a bad idea. she looked frustrated and confused tyring to put things together " sorra i am gettin bits an peaces everythins merging tagether in stages an slowly comin back. seems from yer words i owe ye an apologie i canna remember a the moment why i sought what i were steelin.. last i remember was fighten me father .."

she frowned as immages began crowding in not making much sense at first then becoming clearer she curses and sits up ignroing the broken ribs with a gasp.."where in bloody hell is he. Lachlen ... he kened who i were why did he hide it from me ?"

Vaul waited quietly and paitently he had no idea what had lead up to these events and her being here but he was glad she was returned to herself. "I dont know i fear I had forced him to retreat from here when my rock thrulls started to kill some of the crew..."

The words were apollogetic and solmn "he likly coulnt have gotten to far as he is likly waiting for.. 'Faeril' but you shouldnt worry about such in your state. Luckily neither of us died but the fighting was obviously intense enough to have near made me die from lack of air.

Had your alternate side chosen to use that tactic sooner.." He would smirk slightly in self amusment "and of course to have knocked you out much a sign to your natural luck given that you happened to have been knocked out by one of the over all... 5 or so fiends who wouldnt have killed you or if they had decided to keep you would have been worse."

"i ha news fer ye thas no the worst attack i ha but aye even as Faeril i felt i knew ye an altho i was a pirate as pirates go i wasnna wholly corrupt " grins " i only kill if i had na choice"

"Fair enoughness"

"ach gods i ache.. but tis well deserved..tis strange rememberin.. thins i did as two different people.. isna the same as shiften forms ... tis well i canna discribe it..."

she paused turning her thoughts twords Lachlen.. " he'll most like be waitin as ye say if he dusna ken i ha me memorie back then mayhap i ken get close enough ta beat the truth out o him er i kill him fer keepin the truth from me..."

she wouldnt really kill him not unless he forced her to but damn she was frustrated .. how Adewen, Rhannon, Honnora and the others must be worried, and Vukan she blushed thinking of him and what they had done.

She had no doubt that he would have helped her remember who she was sooner, but what had happened to him... why hadnt he joined her on ship.. he had started to convince her she questions with no answers but would be soon.

"Aye I am glad to see you as your self once more my apolloges our first meeting in so long had to take place in such a bout as this" He would continue to rub his sore throat- "shall i have the imps bring anything for you?"

"ye wouldna ha any rum about would ye ? " she asked only half serious..

He would snap his fingers and an imp would stroll into the room holding a case of various alcohals opening it wide as Vaul grips the first bottle of wine in reach and walks it to her.

Wyn grins up at him and accepts the bottle wincing as each movement brings about more pain but knows in time it will pass." thank ye.."

Lachlen convinced the crew she was dead and that he was now captin taking over her ship they left the realm.

add in vaul and wyn seeking her crew............)

Wyn had left the corpse of her first mate behind having forced air into his lungs and causing them to explode she had watched the blood poor from his eye sockets as the air had forced his eyes to pop from his skull and hadnt cared.

He had refused to tell her anything as to what had happened to Vukan but the others that had helped him upon seeing his end sang like song birds, them she ended quickly with her sword.

she might have been able to forgive him for lieing to her about who she was and keeping it from her, but she wouldnt and couldnt forgive his sellng another into slavery even as the Piarate Faeril she hadnt condonned slavery...

Taking back control of her crew her injuires from facing Vaul. Were healed she wasnt dressed in her ushual style, but rather in Damarian armor which she had not worn sense the battle to free Easur.. Wynwillow prepaired for battle.

Demon slavers wernt ones to be trifled with, and were experts in there craft they had also forged the chins that had once held the Damarians prisoner locating Vukan who had been sold wouldnt be an easy task, but one she was determened to set right.

They had just returned to earth after having taken vaul back to his realm and her ship was landing on the water well out of sight near some isles few knew of where it contantly stormed.. she took on human form and begain giving orders to her crew.

Chapter 14

Jericho smiles as he drinks a bottle of rum slowly, his leather boots on the bar's counter as he leans back in a chair. The town wasn't as deserted as before, there is a collection of Necromancers and other outcasts.

Jericho placed down the bottle as he hears one of the villagers come running in and start speaking of an approaching vessel. Not one to take chances on the wellbeing of Viklin, Jericho gets to his feet and cracks his neck.

Gripping the handle of his blade he quickly runs out of the tavern and runs to the port where The Necropolis is anchored. Crusader seeing his grandson come running with urgency, he weighs the anchor and starts to set course for the vessel after hearing about it approaching from his grandson.

Breaking the clouds Crusader gets a feeling he has seen the ship before. "Fire." Jericho speaks with an angered tone, his rage boiling to the surface as he remembers the last time strangers can close to Viklin, it was a slaughter. With a nod, the cannons start to fire down upon the approaching vessel.

Having been below stalking the ships larder with food stores and water necessary should they set sail soon Morgan a half siren half elf that had just recently joined Jerichos crew was abord when they weghed anchor and set sail.

she came above deck covering her ears just as the cannons roared her purple gem like eyes looking out to see the ship they were firing up on wasnt one she was used to seeing there was something about it the large crystals and such she drew her daggers and prepaired to board when they got close enough to do so ...

Wyn curshed as cannon fire sounded and her top sail busted in two coming down heavly upon the deck her crew mis matched as it was with her son herself lycons vampires and other beings scattered out of the way.

she took on her true form once more and gave the order to prepair the cannons as well as the crystals she intended to channle the energy in them into an electrical attack vurses using them to create a sheild as she turned the wheel brining the ship about to return fire ..-

Jericho growls as he jumps from the ship along with a group of his skeletal crew, some of them armed with an assortment of ranged weapons including crossbows that fire necro energy. drawing his Arwen sword, Jericho crashes down onto the deck of the vessel with a roll and quickly gets to his feet, assuming a fighting posture as he looks about for the captain.

Crusader places the vessel above the other and grips his dragon hammer with a mighty grip, jumping from the railing of the ship he falls through the air like a rock and slams down onto the deck with a mighty crash, his hammer poised to start breaking heads.

Catching sight of the blue fur coloured creature that must be the captain, he breaks into a rapid spring, his blade poised to attack as he jumps and spins his body, swinging his blade with tremendous force towards her ribs.

Seeing a fur creature running towards him with claws poised, Crusader swings his hammer about with might force, the creature barely able to jump back in time before Crusader follows up with a punch to the abdomen, sending the creature back a few steps.

Wyn laughed as she turned to the side avoiding his blade as he aimed for her ribs she blocked and pushed the blade aside with her sword, in one hand her dagger in the other.

stepping up close enough to kiss him if she wished her pink eyes gilttering dangerously she said.." ye picked the wrong ship ta attack lad.. " she brought her head back and then forward intending to head but him hard..

Morgan also boarded and begain to sing her sirens song wich would effect the lycons and sevral other crewmen causing them to drop there wepons and jump overboard into the water.. Wyn was uneffected becasue she created a wind berrier to carrie the sound up and way from her as she fought.

Jericho only smirked as he quickly sidestepped her attack and then went for a knee to the gut, looking as young as he does Jericho is actually over sixty years old his body not able to age past his early twenties due to the necro energy within him.

Crusader growls a undead growl as he swings for the creature again but the creature dodges with cat like grace and kicks Crusader round the jaw hard, forcing him to drop his hammer.

Landing on the deck, the creature sends a flourish of kicks and punches towards Crusader, most of which Crusader is unable to block but he does manage to land a few hits himself.

Wyn was faster than most gave credit for she was there one moment and gone the next having moved back as she felt him adjust his weight to bring his knee up she was looking at him studying him. " nicely done lad bu yell needs be mun faster if yer ta fight me.. somethin about ye seems familiar ta me tho.. ha we met afor ??"

she lept forward brining her sword from lower left up to upper right across his body intending to cut him from hip to sholder her dagger in her other hand she held out and away ready to use it to strike or block as needed ...

Morgan faced one of the crewmen who hadnt been effected ducking under the beings arms brining her own dagger around to slice open his side as the being brought one hand down to his wound she lept up on the rail and jumped up to deliver a side kick to his face then turned to go help Crusader.

"I can't say we have, I'd remember such a pretty face." Jericho speaks with a calm tone as a large appange made of bone shoots out of her back and aims for the shoulder of the arm she holds her blade with.

The bone is tipped sharp and deadly making it perfect for skewering people. Crusader growls as he has had enough, grabbing both of the creature's fists he brings his metal helmet done, colliding with the bare skull of the creature.

The sound of black steel again bone would echo as Crusader throws the creature up into the air and then punches his chest with great force, sending the disorientated creature into the railing. Crusader steps a moment to see if the creature is alive before he roars out in pain, a blade had piercing his blade from one of the other crewmen.

Seeing her sword cut into the captin who was attacking her ship and crew was a short lived satisfaction as at the same time bone shot from him and into the sholder of the arm that had held her dagger the nerve damage causing her to drop the blade.

"well played lad were both wounded .. but play time be oer.. i ha mur thins ta do then ye ken fathom.. " Wyn with drew from him pulling her self from the bone impailing her sholder and stepping back removing her sword from him.

she gathered energy about her and the wind picked up a sworling of air growing about the deck what was left of her crew knew to take cover the whorl wind gathered strenght and moved threw out the ship pulling the skelingtons into it that wernt smart enough to hold fast sweepting them out to sea..

Wyn flew up into the air putting distance between them looking for her son wishing to see where he was in all this when Crusader caught her attention.. .. just as crusader sent a crewman flying a woman in a hat with long flowing white hair and purple eyes joined him.

Wyn didnt know who she was but was clearly apart of the other crew .. but something about crusader caught her attention.. and held it fast causing her to call out ..” ENOUGH! “ as they stopped to look at her puzzled she glide down to land before him..

Jericho mentally cursed as he fell to his chest, this was the side effect of being a Necromancer he couldn’t feel by normal means. His vision darkens slowly as he feels himself slipping into the abyss of death.

Crusader pulls the blade from him and growls as he stares at the creature before him through his helmet, something about her was familiar but that was cut short as he quickly turned to see Jericho bleeding out. “GRANDSON!” Crusader yells out in a decayed voice breaks into a sprint, knocking out all others in his way.

“i ken heal him.. bu in return ye mun stop attacken me ship.. do ye agree ?”

Crusader says nothing as he walks over to a dead member of Wyn’s crew and slams his fist into the corpses chest, a eerie green glow would surround Crusader as he points his finger at Jericho.

The energy of the soul being drained from the corpse, passed through Crusader and into Jericho. Jericho gasps as he feels his necro-energy charging, his body healing on its own while he feels the power of the soul through him, he has yet to master his powers.

Wyn sheathed her wepons as Morgan came up to her. Morgan was thinking that now that the wind had died down if this creature could heal her captin she would force her compliance by using her sirens song.

seeing crusader had there captin well in hand thought perhaps if she could take control of the captin they wouldnt need to fight for the ship any longer.. " ye are familiar ta me.. i has seen this like afor lon ago.. well oer a hundred years er so.. .... tis been a long while me frien bu how did ye die ??"

as Morgan begain to sing Wyns eyes glittered dangerously as she shook off the effects and silenced Morgans singing by cutting off her air.." Dunna test me lass.. i am na some human salor er lesser bein such as a lycon er vampire a fall fer such"

Releaseing her Wynwillow watched her gasp for air on the deck of her ship.. before turning her eyes turned back at Crusader and his grandson.." nor am i as soft er weak as i once were..."

"Thanks Crusader." Jericho smiles softly before a heavy punch from Crusader sends Jericho flying beside Feral Wyn's son, but with a smile on his face. "DON'T SCARE ME LIKE THAT GRANDSON!" Crusader yells as Jericho bursts out into laughter.

Wyn looked over at Crusader and gave him a cheeky grin and nod before moving to one of her crewmens side.." why did ye attack us.. did ye no recognize me ship ? ye did help me come up wi the design ta gi Rhannon fer the buildin o it .." Wyn was speaking to Crusader she brought one hand up to her sholder to try and stem some of the blood flow.

"My memory is not as it used to be and I must say it was Jericho's order to attack." Jericho chuckles as he jumps to his feet and runs at Crusader with tremendous speed, sending a right hook to his Grandfather's face and sending him into the railing. "Viklin doesn't welcome strangers now, not after the slaughter brought on by the Orients."

Feral couldn't help but rolls his eyes as he shakes his head at his mother, he had been adopted by Wyn and she had accepted him trained him and looked after him when able he knew her more as Faeril then as Wyn.

However he was coming to know her as she is now and learning now more about the Damarains and Easur as well. Slowly getting to his feet he grabs onto the railing.

Wynwillow rested a hand on his sholder as she spoke to him " gettin slow on me son ? were gonna ha ta up yer trainin.." she said teasing her him a bit having seen him roll his eyes. Morgan finnaly recovered her breath enough to stand glaring at Wyn..

"i am na a stranger here lad i helped yer granda lon ago i used ta call these isles home an en helped brin merchets an such here once least wise till they turned agains me in fear .. " humph.. humans .. ahh well that were a long while ago i supose.. canna expect ta be remembered .. still.. im hurt ye didna remember me me frien.."

"Death does that, I'm afraid if not for Jericho here I would not be here to see you." Crusader says as Crusader grits his teeth. "years ago the Orients turned against us and slaughtered my Grandfather, I was only ten when I brought him back as what he is." Jericho says as Crusader removes his helmet and mask.

Wynwillow bows politely then walks up to crusader and hugs him..she cant help grinning tho as she says.." wha is i wi the undead havin green hair .."

"Well, he may be the last soon, I'm living on borrowed time." Jericho says which makes his grandfather glare daggers at him, but it is true. Jericho wasn't ready for his powers and thus, he has to absorb the souls of defeated enemies to remain alive lest he falls to ash.

Morgan gasped at this not having known that but otherwise remained silent.. Wyn nodded..” im glad i go ta see ye en if ye did attack me once more afor ye do go.. im sorra i wasna here ta aid ye when the time came ken ye fergi me”

“It’s not your fault Wyn besides, the Orients will pay in time.” Jericho had gone silent as he thinks upon his life, looking a little lost within his eyes as Crusader walks over to him and hands him a medallion of sorts. “You remember what we are don’t you Grandson?” Crusader asks with a calm tone and Jericho nods, pulling a similar necklace from under his vest.

“i mun be off once i fish me crew out o the sea what be left o them an repairn the damage done.. have ye heard any roomers o a slaver ship hear abouts an im no talkin the human kind..”

“Didn’t one of the scouts report seeing a slaver ship occupied with demons heading for Orient waters?” Crusader says to Jericho with a curious tone but only for Jericho to jump to his feet and start shouting to his skeletal crew.

“BACK ONTO THE NECROPOLIS BOYS! I’VE HAD ENOUGH OF WAITING TO DIE, TIME TO SPILL SOME ORIENT BLOOD!” The skeletal crew roar and raise their blades into the air before ropes hit the deck from above, the skeletal crew clambering up the ropes back to the ship.

Wyn chuckles.. “ mind if me son an i join ye fer a wee while ? if the one im seekin be aboard i owe him his freedom.. the battle with the slaver ship they caught up to had been a short lived one as it was not the ship Wyn sought.

it wasnt entirely a human slave ship but nore was it the demons she was seeking the crew had been a mixture of lycons vampires and such similar to wyns own crew but slavers instead..

she thanked Crusader and Jericho and once returned to her ship she and her crew made the repaires needed.. she hugged Crusader once more and when he asked where she would go next Wyn simply smiled.

"i go ta Adewen in the main land ta the west i needs inform her o what has happened sense i ha me memorie back an ta re supplie me ship.. an after tha well then i go ta fin an free Vukan.."

Chapter 15

Wyn entered Adewens tavern on the main land and was nearly knocked over as Adewens head quickly came up locating her threw the crowed. Her silvery eyes locking with Wyn's pink ones as she called out Wynwillows name running to her weaving threw the crowed of patrons to hug her fearcly and tightly.

"Where have you been we've all been worried about you you must tell me all that happened.." Wyn grinned aware they were drawing attention she said.." aye all in good time how er how bout a draught o rum an well go above ta yer office an i'll explain all ye ken.."

Adewen looked around smiled and nodded her agreement ordering food as well as drink to be brought above stairs. Took Wynwillow's hand and lead her up the stair well into her office.. " now explain.."

Wynwillow explained everything that had happened sense she had left Easur last telling Adewen about the crystal the council had thought distroyed by the demons when they had invaded why she had gone after it to ether bring it back or distroy it.

"ye see i didna want ye er the others ta be counted as accomplises should i fall inta the wrong hands.. i couldna risk thos on the council removin thos who aided me .. i had ta distroy it.."

“when me da heard me former crew talkin abou the crystal the old captin an i had hidden me da put two an two tagether an took his own band the DarkOaks Damarians he had gathered like idri had who had escaped..”

“They went after it ta use it as a wepon.. tis how i lost me memorie... “ she went on to tell Adewen about meeting Vukan in the tavern as Faeril, contining on into how she had recovered her memeorie and what had happened to Vukan..

Adewen listened and didnt inetrupt shaking her head on occasion until she had finnished.. “one you shouldnt have gone alone we would have helped you we love you. You daft woman.. but were glad your back and safe.

as well as that Vaul is once again awake and among us perhpas one day he will visit Easur again.. and before you go again there are a few young Damarians teens by humans standereds who are here on earth they would be benifical one is of your own family branch..”

Wyn grinned and agreed to take them knowing if she didnt then Adewen would go with her herself..”aye who may i be taken wi me.. an where do i fin them..? “ Adewens silvery eyes glittered with humor as they met Wynwillows.

Both knowing the other extreamly well having worked beside each other many times.. “ they are here in the tavern actually they arrived only a few days ago and have been exploring Killian of the Druidoaks, Adeon of the DragonBanes and Merden of the Firelights.. im suprised you didnt pick up there scents when you entered..”

Wyn nodded a small frown on her face “ aye i am suprised as well tha i didna.. wha be there skills be they ready fer this?, tis no easy task ahead o me Ade. i go after demon slavers no just ..”

Adewen held her hand up looking angry and cutting off her words. “ Trust me Wyn they are capable i taught and trained them myself while you were away playing pirate...”

it was Wyns turn to look angry she set the empty rum tankered down and stood intending to head for the door she had her hand on the door latch when Adewen called to her.

“Wait... “ Wynwillow paused..” i apologise memorie loss cant be helped it was wrong of me to say such.. will you take them ? “ Wyn turned back to face her..

“aye i’ll take um ..” Wyn said no more simply bowed politely and a bit mockingly from one previous council member to another Adewens silvery eyes glittlered dangerously.

Adewen was aware Wynwillow wasnt bowing to show respect as they would often do twords one another but more mockingly.. and threw her ink well at the door as Wyn walked out of it.

The inkwell shattered against the door as it closed behind Wyn. Adewen shook her head as she heard Wynwillow chuckling as she went down the stairs a slight grin touching her own lips it was good to have Wyn back.

Wyn made her way down the stairs and sought out Killian, Adeon, and Merden she hugged Killian and shook the other twos hands taking them off to the side, and to one of the back tables.

Once they introduced themselves and they reolized who she was they quietly begain to discuss the mission she was going on with them.

Merden Firelight as Vukan was one of his kinsmen was more then happy to help with the task, and also asked to bring one other along. Vukans sister Laila who was on earth.

He stepped out with Wyn’s permission to use one of the crystals to communicate with her she was only a few leauges away and so flying to them wouldnt take long to reach them..

Laila had many questions and was very angry with Wynwillow, but also understood not all of what had happened was Wyns fault.

However as Wyn was trying to set right what had gone wrong as well as killed the men responsable Laila was willing to forgive her to an extent and would indeed join them in freeing her brother.

Adewen came back down stairs after contacting the rest of the council and updating them on Wynwillows status, and informing them that Wyn was taking others with her to free Vukan.

She went back to running the tavern occasionaly stoping to visit with Wyn and the others greeting Laila happy to see her as well insisitng they remain the night at the tavern/inn.

They headed out in the morning giving Wyn's new crew a night's rest, and time to restalk the ship. They agreed and rested the night..

Wyn, Laila, Killian, Adeon, and Merden returned to her ship at first light weghing anchor they set sail until they were well away from the humans line of sight before the ship began rising out of the water and into the sky to open a rift the search for Vukan now fully underway..

....

The sea breeze was rash and rough the night air thick with the spray of crashing waves upon the 'Hanged mermaid' a well crafted ship famous for the linage of scoundrals whom served on it.

A short man sleek framed man with skin touched regulerly by the sun as was clear from his tanned complextion cast honey colored eyes upon the horizen holding himself in place at the center of the deck with an armored arm coiled in ropes holding the sails wide open as slight grin forming upon his silver ring periced lips as his points with his free hand at the Horizen calling out

"Men look you there! some see land on the Horizen but I see the glimmer of gold as we bring in our ample payload!" -he men gave a hearty cruel cheer before getting eagerly back to work the idea of spending thier share on the finest whores and drink the docks had to offer all the motivation they needed.

Wyn spoke to the crew at large as well as to thos goin inland with her.." i think our best bet o locatin wether er no Vukan be here be fer some o ye ta change yer forms.."

"i ken go in as shadow tis a drow form i ha used afor.. an i ken change me voice.. dunna dra attenion ta yerselfs but blend in as much as yer able..."

"i ha coin a pelnty ta try an buy him but if i am able then we will take him back by force an flee we needs agree on some sort o signal..only Vaul, Merden, Adeon, an meself will go ashore the rest o ye will keep the ship ready should we needs flee quickly.."

she looked to Vual then as she changed her form.. " what do you suggest my friend..? " she changed her voice and accent to match the form she had taken so as to complete her disguise. Merden, Adeon and Laila changed forms as well taking on verious demons shapes sizes and so forth..

The salt of the air was pungent from the spray each breth soaked in its taste as the storm began to subside the clouds of a storm having already passed the docks of Jastur one of the more infamous locals in this realm of Vagabonds and cut throats but filled to the brim with 'customers and property'

Both in the eyes of the slavers but for this batch of thier load they had a very particuler buyer in mind. The short tanned man with a head shved to the skin giving him a hairless appearance save for the well trimmed light blond colored brows resting over his hungry honey colored eyes one of the men calling out.

"Oui! commander Hult what ye gonna spend ye share on?" The tanned man with honey eyes identified as Hult snickered as the ship slowly settled into port as he was the first to leap from the ship to the dock his outfit of cain mail inter woven with black cloth and dark tanned leather and a arm length iron gauntlet clanging and jingling as he ties off the ropes.

“you dont worry about my share just get them pieces of property off the ship our buyer isnt the patiant sort and we have lots of little slaves and our one special to make presentable by noon” as the words are sead the sun peaks over the seas horizen marking the morning.

Wyn directed Mearden to scout the right half of the area they had time before the auctions would begin they would take up various positons around the area coming in from different angles so as not to draw too much attention.

Adeon she sent to the left Laila she kept with her making there way twords the center and the fights that would be held before and after the auctions for enertainment..

Wyn in the form of a drow called Shadow, a form she had taken a time or two before walked among them. A few taking notice of her. One who dared try to grab her ass instantly had his wrist twisted and snapped a dagger held at his thoat as she hissed telling him did he try it again he would have more then a broken wrist to nurse.

she released him a the sound of other demons laughing at his plight and placed her arm over Laila who was disugised as well clearly stating to all as she swept the crowed with her gaze hands off .. before moving back threw the crowd no further advances being made to ether of them.

Several armed men in the gaurds of raiders strided off the ship the survivors of failed crews they had signed up with the slavors to serve as extra muscle for thier dealings a fact that made Hult more at ease.

The raiders forming groups of two and standing at intervals upon the pathway from the docks to thier location a fair sized abandoned building once belonging to a curropt merchant who cheated one to many clients.

After the raiders had taken thier place thier pressence a sign to the less ruthless inhabotant of the port to keep thier distance making the way clear as the slaves as marched out of the ship ship connected in a procession line of sorrow tight metal collars on very slaves throat.

The rest of the crew were active as well several slave tamers walked with the procession as firm whip in hand harshly crackin on the back of any slave who dared slow down the march of which there would be many out of this cargo of 234 still living pieces of soon to be human property.

Hult watched everything from the sides making sure everything was on schedual the expectations of thier Major buyer on the line and he would have nothing slow down the proceedings as he yelled with a harsh short tempered call

"Hurry it up you filthy moving tools! and I swear the first of you who causes me grief will get thier skin flayed open and they will be wallowed in the salts of the sea before thier beating as well as they will loose the clothign we have so graciously given you!"

Adeon had wondered threw the area checkin out the verious actiivitys watching quietly as a fist fight broke out among one set of men the others gathering around to watch before moving on Merden did the same save he watched a dice game and verous other gamblings.

Laila and Shadow watched the fights in the ring but everyones attention was gained as the slaves were brought threw all of them watching to see what they could and size up which they may want to buy if the leader dosnt pick them..

Vukans tall blue winged form was easly spotted among them.. he looked a bit rough around the edges and as if hed taken a beating or two the blood on the chains he wore around the cuffs let them know he had fought agaisnt them and tryed to ether escape or remove them at one point.

The marks from the lashes had healed human slow as there hadnt ben another there to heal him.. Wyn's eyes narrowed as she tryed not to think about what he had suffered to keep her fetures schooled looking assessing rather than concerned.

The procession moved quickly underway the slaves were taken with minimum incident no one dared to invoke Hult's threat and only a few suffered the tamers lash due to thier feable condition.

After a while all of the slaves had reached thier desintation the abandoned home of a merchant waiting to become the living property of whoever decided to spend thier coin on them.

The non tamer or raider crew got quick at work filling buckets with very lightly soaped cold water making all of the slaves huddle together before they would douse them with the chilly liquid.

The human and other mundane species amongst the slaves all shivering as Hult commands his hedge mage hired years earlier to handle events which steel simple would not suffice for the mage.

a quick motion to aim his hands at the pubbles under the slaves turning it to a piller of hot steam to clean and make the slaves presentable if very worn and at the edge of burns.

Hult yawns the all night voyage was getting to him but his eyes would never stay closed for longer than a blink at least not until the auction was done.

"Get all these slaves primed and ready for the auction I intend to get all the gold thier worth and they had best be presentable enough that the 'Buyer' we came to this port to sell to had beetter not be dissapointed"

He walked over to table where some of the raiders and slavers sat eating dried fish, and cabbage fine meal for one so accustom to the see as he was.

Vaul had listened to the plan to simply purchase Vukan's freedom but he did not agree with the prospect he knew scum and vagabonds, and all manner of lesser men like these and he knew Vukan would be sold only for top coin or only to special parties.

So concealed with Coal colored cloak not noticed in the crowds as he carfully hid his face, and horns Vaul had slipped into the ports square center where the slaves would be auctions.

Quickly slipped into the first abandoned second story room his eyes could find, but forcing him to kill two addicts to prevent his discovery Vaul waited and watched with his extended perception to see what occured.

They all made there way to the acution building knowing that as soon as it was possable it would start she motioned for Laila to remain at the back while she took the front area many would be scrambling for the best place for a closer look.

she wanted them scattered to better be able to aid one another in escaping if necessary one fellow came up to her placing his arm around her sholders. " well well well what have we here a lovely peacie you be. wanna go have some fun before the bidding starts if your lookin fer a plesure slave i'll be yours for free no need to waist your coin."

Shadow smiled up at him just as one of his mates who had seen her break the other fellows wrist earler called out to him.. " careful that one's got claws " but that one warning was too late by then she brought her knee up into his groin a slow grin touching her lips as his compaions advanced.

she held a dagger to his doubled over form and drew her sword with the other as she spoke..sounding as board as she possably could..his men paused and watched her closely " your not worth the effort it would take to clean my blades of your blood let alone to join me in my bed.."

she removed her dagger and kicked him over waving his men over with her sword still in hand his men nodded to her and helped him to his feet moving back well away from her sevral others staying out of reach as well even after she sheathed her blades. The man she had kneed vowing to pay her back as his companions took him away.

Hult stood at the edge of the Lawn of the house which opend into the ports center lifting his unarmored hand to his lips and blowing out a long attention drawing whistle the signal that the event was to Begin.

as 25 fair cuilaity humans all of moderate age and helth are dragged to be presented to the crowd. After that batch of Humans 2 Lycan, 5 dwarfs, and 12 elves were marched out to stand behind them.

they all take thier position Hult turns to the crowd and grins taking a step back as a well dressed member of the slavers wearing silken robes and gaudy trinkets walks out and announces with the voice of a professional.

"Ladies and gentlemen we have before you our first batch of slaves for the evening these are all top quiality and will serve well for any of the mercinary or assassin group looking for raw recruits this lot already knows to shut up when there betters speak."

The 2 Lycans hang thier head in shame they had fought to remain free but had lost that will and so were resigned to this fate as the other merly looked forward emotionless these were the slaves whom had known the tamers fury and knew nothing but slavery now.

Shadow bid on the two lycons as did others in the crowed and let herself get outbid. Adeon bet on one of the elven women. Mearden one of the Dwarves and Laila one of the male elves, and even a human male.

Each driving the bids up but eventally letting another bidder win out there was only one they were interested in but shadow/wyn had a feeling they were saving him for last or for someone specail..

Hult smiled as the batch of well kept and will broken slaves had made him enough money to make up for all the coasts of thier last several months at sea and yet the best was yet to come. The next batch were more exotic creatures 5 mermaids with a hedge mage.

standing in a shadow cast by the building using mist to keep them hydrated while they were held up to be seen by all. The mermaids and mage were followed by a band of young energetic imps, a siren, and finaly 7 drows. when all were in place Hult grinned and gestured out to the crowd "do I hear any offers on these fine pieces of property?"

Adeon Bid on the merfolk and the sirens cursing and grumbling as if he were truly pissed at being outbidden Merden bid on a few of the Nymphs grunting only when out bid tho frowning.

Shadow and Laila bid on the Drow Shadow being Wyn feeling a bit bad at having to let herself be out bid on them she had an afinity for the drow as her disguise would indicate.

she had to remind herself they couldnt save everyone and they would need all they had to try and get Vukan if indeed he was presented and there leader hadnt kept him for himself.

Hult smirked so many people betting upon the merchandise jumped its value immensly it looked like a this would make the whole crew quite wealthy and yet there was one last batch for this port with the rest already promised to a Lord with a large farm in the west.

"Ladies and gentlemen we have come to the highlight of the evning with several specialties brought to you all here for your pleasure!" finaly three lesser fiends of Nifleheim were marched into view.

thier wills were still strong but thier chains made them so weak and thier malnurished bodies shook with rage, 10 Amazons all vicious and visably angry but thier will was dimmed by mental signs of punishment.

7 Gargoyles to stupid to know what resistance was when others yelled at them, and finaly 2 Damarians one Vukan battered but not without the strength to stand, and the other a woman slightly older who looked down at the ground with shame obvciously some escaped survivor of the attack on Esuar whom had remained hidden until captured by the slavers.

Hult grinned and gestured "do note that all of these slaves require a stronger hand than most have, we are not responisble for the slaves actions after purchase, and we will be putting a limit upon our special catch the damairans only one can be purchased the other will be saved for a individual who has the money and right to demand one of them"

Shadow nearly gave herself away in her shock at not only seeing Vukan but a female Damarian as well her eyes narrowed and her arms crossed.

Only one able to be purcheced, she wanted to know who these slavers had right to demand anyone as a slave let alone a damarian. No this would not due however they could only save one at a time they were out numbered.

it took all her will power to appear to be asessing all the ones presented and not simply let loose her temper and fight right then. she sense the tension in the others as well but smiled.

appearing to any looking at her as if she had come to a decision on who she would bid on when in truth it was because the others hadnt given themselves away ether.. now the real bidding would begin..

Chapter 16

It took time for the others to be sold they were specialty goods but all have thier own uniqe Value. Vaul alone could hardly stand it all stitting there with barly contained grief from his hinding spot as he imagined the pride of his fellow fiends being taken from them one by one.

it was the sight of the other Damarian that sparked something in him words of his own uttered years past that echoed deep in his soul. “I promised to let the Damarians see thier home... I promised it to Idrialla...I wont have my word loose its value”

there was a black blur in the air as Vaul leaped from his hiding spot the air crackling with his power as his hand griped hight hot with aura already sundering the chains before it could stops his hands freeing instantly the lesser fiends whom grined with delight and leapt upon the crowd.

Eager to regain their vigor with slaughter and feast. the chains for the others were loosened but remained hanging upon them as Vaul turned to the wide eyed hedge mage out streching his right hand sending forth a tendral that gripped the mages head and squished it in its grasp

Hult cursed he had seen attempts to free slaves before but never had such a display of power been aimed at them as he saw here and now lifting his ungauntleded hand to his lips and letting out a ear blistering whistle.

Catching the raiders attention and snapping them out of thier shocked haze as they grabed thier weapons and moved to surround the slaves and the rampaging fiends and thier would be savior.

As soon as Vaul reached the stage Wyn and the others went into action sheading there disugises Wyn leaping upon the stage near Vaul using her sword forged of damarian steel and enchanted dragonscales not to cut the chains.

she was well aware of there ability to nullafy magics but at the pins holding the chains to the shackles in place so that the rest of the slaves who were still bound. Were able to at least run. As she did this Vaul killed the Hedge mage and she heard the whistle of the one who had been running the auction.

Adeon Mearden and Laila were helping the Fiends Vaul had freed thin out the crowed so they would have less to contend with using there elements, and weopons, but also keeping a wary eye on the fiends should they decide to attack one of them by mistake.

Wyn while the raiders snaped out of there shock advanced on Hult used her air abilitys to do two things at once. One silence him by robbing him of air, and two to manipulate the air currents sending up a wave of air blowing some of the raiders who had made there way up to the stage off of it.

They flew back to land in the middle of the frey she trusted Vaul to have her back. Laila fought her way to her brothers side, and handed him a wepon tho bound she knew he could still fight with a blade. The female they didnt know what her skills were yet so Merden joined Laila and helped protect Vukan and the female Damarian.

Vaul was in a trance common to his kind his eyes locking from one major detail to the next his hand outstreching and sending forth tiny bolts of his aura like a small storm of Ominous and arrow volly in every direction.

each one striking at the chains of those whom had been bought at auction the Lycans, humans, elves, dwarfs, Mermaids, drow, Imps, were suddenly freed though Vaul quivered his head dizzy as he grined and looked to Wynwillow.

"Sorry for loosing myself lady Wyn I fear I am not as patiant as I would wish, but at least we get some excitment now" Vaul looked to one of the tamers trying to reel back his whip to stop the advancing humans but Vaul lept upon the man.

Both of his fiendish hands upon the tamers throat squeezing the life from him for a moment before suddenly snapping his neck with a cringe worthy cracking sound the slaves now freed taking whatever they could find to use as weapons.

Hult cursed as he saw the the slaves freed one by one only to not be stoped by the tamers as they were slaughtered knowing well that even in their state of mal nurishment the slaves would be out for vengance and blood.

The slaves who had lost thier will suddenly looked down at thier freed hands and trembled as they heard a far off cry "If you will be slaves then put upon yourself chains if you would be free then know yourself to be alive and worthy to live!"

They looked to see the words coming from Vaul whom was ripping his claw into the flesh of another tamer. The slaves took heart to this especily the Lycans who with bloodlust and rampage leapt upon the crew whom had jeered and beaten them endless times.

Wyn grinned at Vauls words tho her attention was fully on the one infront of her Hult tho she knew not his name it was not her however who delivered the killing blow but Vukan.

Vukan had for but a few moments been swamped by so many emotions the hated feeling of the chains of being sold of being beaten. His head had come up and hope had flared in his heart at the sight of Vaul and then Wyn upon the stage.

Along with the scents of the other damarians as they had joined the frey and love as well as relif and fear at knowing his sister was present. Shame at them seeing him like this but mostly.. anger so much anger..at the situation.

The slavers and at Wyn he had accpeted the wepon given him by his sister they fought along side the others protecting the female Damarian she hadnt spoken to him while imprisoned.

He had a feeling she was suprised to see him as much as he had been her and suspeted she knew nothing of her own kind. That would now be remidied. As soon as his chains were off he turned on Wyn who was facing his captor and tormentor.

He was tempted to use his ability with fire on them both, after all she had put him here sent him to this hell. He shook with the anger he felt the sense of betrayal by her.

He kept control of himself she had come to help free him after all, and so focused his rage on Hult. Engulfing him in flames that burned brighter and hotter wrapping around him.

At first from his feet up to his ankles like a snake winding round its prey before devouring him and covering him completely turning blue and then a pure white leaving behind if anything nothing but ash.

in its wake before he dropped to his knees having nearly drained himself to the point of blacking out Wynwillow had stopped her attack. as the flames spread and backed away the others began to run no longer willing to stay and fight at least for the present.

Wyn reached out to Vukan after he dropped to his knees meaning to offer comfort.." Dont.. Dont touch me.. i dont want you near me.. " Vukan looked at her his eyes filled with such hate it hurt to see such pain.

altho she had not given the orders for him to be sold she had thought he had just changed his mind but that was no excuse she was in part at fault.

Wyn stepped back lowering her hands to her sides she had feared this would be the result.. Laila spoke.." Vukan she didnt know, and as soon as she found out she set out to save you.." he looked up hate in his eyes..

"her ship .. her crew.. she was captin.. " Wyn simply nodded not explaining anything for she doubted he would listen.." Laila if ye'll help him ta the ship we can take as many as till hold an ge everyone out o here..."

Laila looked like she wanted to argue more but thought her brother needed to heal physicly before they could work on the menatal and took him to the ship once there began the healing.

Adeon and Merden going with her, the female damarian following not sure where else to go only having heard that those who had freed them were offering passage.. Wyn remained where she was unmoving.

When the dust cleared and all was done Vaul glared at Vukan dissapointed at his behavior but would let it pass so long as he controled his own actions standing around Vaul were the fiends still thin and weak but healthier than they were mere moments ago.

full of the sweet meats of their captors and torturers cackiling and standing at the ready by the ones whom had freed them the other slaves either rejoiced or wept with joy at the scene in its entirity thier freedom had been given them.

when they were resigned to lives of eternal servitude to be nothing more than property. The crows and citizens whom had escaped the massacre had scrambled to thier homes not eager to get in the path of the slaves or the ones who freed them.

Vaul heard the command to load up the freed slaves onto the ship and looked over to the three lesser fiends "Go and tell the others they can get on a ship with us to leave this port in an hour then I want you three to personaly carry aboared any wounded including her"

He points to the Other damrain whom had nearly become a slave her wings were ripped while she was in the slavers grasp and she had recived a cut to the thigh in the fight so she could not flee. The female Damarian shook her head at them and brought up a hand waiving the fiends back tho injured and moving slow she was making her way to the ship just fine.

The lesser fiends were quick to act eager to do the bidding of a greater fiend of the likes of Vaul who walked over to wyn and smirked resting a hand on her shoulder "Let get back to the ship and have some wine to celebrate ehh?"

Wynwillow looked up at Vaul when his hand came to rest on her sholder tears had gathered in her eyes tho they had yet to fall for she refused to let them, but it seemed no matter how hard she tryed.

They came all the same and for a moment she let herself be weak and wrapped Vaul in a hug hidding her face against his chest only the shaking of her sholders and the slight dampness on his vest from her silent tears were the only indacatrors she was greaving for the loss of what might have been.

After a regianing some control she spoke still not looking up from his chest. her voice was muffled and even more garbled sounding then ushual " en if he kens the truth. hel ner beleive i killed them because o wha they did ta him. He'll simply say i killed them fer there disloyalty..ta there captin sa.. hel ner beleive the truth."

she laughed a bit sounding like a bit of a mad woman but in truth shed rather laugh it off and keep moving forward than continue to sit on her arse and cry for crying wouldnt change a thing.

she then stepped back looking up at Vaul again and wiped away the tears saying “. lets go ha tha drink.. we ha reason enough ta celebrate in tha we freed no only Vukan bu all here an ha foun a lost kinsmen ta boot..”

Vaul stood there silent as she had cried gently hugging her for he knew sadness though it was not natural to him he still could sympathize that Wyn obviously needed his friendship right now and smiles when she looked up at him wiping away her tears as he nodded lightly.

“aye we deserve that, a hardy drink with all the good we have done regardless of how many wanted postures o me face, and yer’s there will be in this port alone by the morrow.” Vaul replyed teasingly sounding something like Wyn.

He smirks and begins the walk torwards the ship as he smiles seeing many of the slaves begining to come as well hoping to get out of this city as quicky as possible.

Wyn laughed at Vauls words a true laugh the glint of mischevious humor reaching her eyes wanted posters were nothing new to her tho most thought of her as Faeril, and rarely did she take the Drow form of Shadow so tho there would be wanted posters of that form of herself she wouldnt be found.

she feared the voyage home would be a long one both she and Vukan had there pride and she gathered hers about her knowing nether would give. she just hoped one day he would forgive her for what he thought she had done. she linked her arm threw Vauls a grave expression on her features, but a determined one.

They made there way to the ship as captin she would have much more to think about and do to occupy her time that would keep her mind from Vukan and what had passed..she wouldnt hide in her cabin, time to get the ship underway and out of this realm.. it was time she thought.. time to return these beings to where they belong, and then home.

Printed in the United States
By Bookmasters